Chosen by the Dragon

Selena Scott

Contents

PROLOGUE

"Come on, Beverly. You can frickin do this," Lucy whispered under her breath as she watched the older woman tremble on one foot.

Lucy wanted to reach out and steady her, but she knew it would mean more to Bev if she did it on her own. With a little groan, Beverly gripped the rails on either side of her and shifted her weight, stepping fully on her other foot.

"Hell yes!" Lucy whooped and couldn't stop herself from hopping up and down. "Bev, you did it!" She helped the woman ease back into the chair behind her. It was her first full step since she'd tripped and broken her leg two months before. Beverly stared up at Lucy; disbelief, joy, and fatigue all materializing on her face.

"I can't believe it, Lucy. I thought I might never- that I would be in the chair f-forever." The woman's voice broke as she finally gave words to the fear that had been plaguing her for weeks. She proudly wiggled her toes before reaching up and clasping Lucy's hands.

It was moments like those that had Lucy coming to work every day. Not every patient was as lucky as Bev, but Lucy made sure they all worked just as hard, and healed as well as their bodies possibly could. She kneeled down and pulled Bev into a hearty hug.

"Bev, that was the shit. Now let's do it again."

The two women grinned at one another, their joy filling the whole room.

Amos couldn't tear his eyes away from this woman, Lucy's radiant face. But he quickly straightened up as he realized he was leaning toward the television screen where they watched her.

"That's her?" King Dalyer asked from beside Amos, his voice dripping with skepticism.

"What?" The Oracle looked up from the game he was playing on his cell phone. He squinted at the television screen on which he'd summoned up the feed of the woman at her work. "Oh. Yeah, that's her."

"But she's so ordinary," the King said.

King Dalyer wasn't dumb. Actually he was searingly smart. But that was the dumbest thing Amos had ever heard someone say. Ordinary? The woman on the screen was hot as fuck.

"Shit!" A sad womp womp sound came from the Oracle's phone and he jammed it back in his pocket. Seeming to remember that he was currently performing a duty for the most powerful being in the human or dragon realm, he turned back to the television screen.

"You think she's ordinary?" The Oracle scratched his stubbly blonde beard. "I think she's kinda cute."

Again, really dumb. Amos thought. Even in her loose scrubs, this woman was like walking viagra. Not that dragon shifters ever had to take viagra.

"Well," the King said as he tossed his hands up in the air. "If that human is really my only option, I'll just have to make do. How do we get to her?"

The Oracle stared dully at a space about a foot in front of him and swiped a finger over his temple a few times, like he was scrolling through information he didn't need. Images flew past on the television screen.

"She lives... here," he said and a dingy brownstone appeared on the screen.

"Brooklyn?"Amos guessed and both the King and the Oracle turned and looked at him in surprise, as if they'd forgotten he was even there. It was one of the things that made Amos such a good bodyguard, being able to disappear in a room.

"Yeah," the Oracle responded. "Which makes it a lot easier to get her to the dragon realm, considering the portal is less than 5 miles away."

He did the temple scroll again and brought up another image on the screen. Free tickets to an art show at a museum in Queens.

The King turned to the Oracle and raised an inquisitive eyebrow, asking what the tickets were for.

The Oracle shrugged. "She's into art. And that museum is three blocks from the portal. I made sure she got the tickets this morning. She's planning on going." The Oracle's eyes unfocused. "No, wait. She decided to go to the bar with her friend Courtney. No, wait, she's back to going to the art show. No. Wait."

The King tossed his hands up in frustration.

"Ok, she's definitely going to the art show." The Oracle leaned in to stage whisper. "Apparently Courtney hasn't been the greatest friend lately."

Amos rolled his eyes and focused back in on the King. The Oracle was too much for him. Useful, sure. But worth the trouble? Nah.

"Fine." The King's voice was sharp as he turned to Amos. "Just make sure she gets here as unscathed as possible. I need her here by the harvest moon."

"Harvest moon?" Amos asked, the date seemed arbitrary to him.

"A dragon can only get a human pregnant on a harvest moon," the Oracle clarified.

"Be careful with getting her here, Amos. I need her in perfect breeding condition," said King Dalyer.

Amos's eyes froze on the woman's face as it all tumbled over him once again, like cold water down his back. He thought about exactly why they were plotting to snatch this woman out of her life. Shit, out of her entire realm. So that King Dalyer could mate with her.

CHAPTER ONE

You win, hair. Lucy thought as she gave up trying to knot it on her head. She dropped her hands and her curly black hair sprang all down her back. She could never get it to do that fancy twist thing that actresses did for the red carpet. Not for a lack of trying. She wanted to look nice for the art show, and, she guessed, for Dale. But mostly for the art show.

He was gonna be here any minute and she knew he'd be pissed if she was late again. No, not pissed, she corrected herself. Disappointed. Dale didn't't get angry. He just got quiet. And then the next time they got together he'd have another self help book for her to read. Gifts, he called them. So far she'd cracked the spines on exactly zero of them. But all stacked up they made a great footrest for watching TV.

"Lucy!"

She heard Dale's voice holler up to her apartment from the street and she winced. He was gonna give her shit about getting her doorbell fixed again. He was always on her about calling her Superintendent for all the fixes her shabby apartment needed. But her Super, Kristof, was like 99 years old and she'd always felt bad asking him to come all the way out to Brooklyn.

Giving her dress one last pull in the mirror, Lucy knew she looked good. Royal blue always made her light eyes look even brighter. And the dress hugged her generous curves.

"Lucy!" he called up through her window again.

His annoyed voice made her jump as she wiggled into her heels and locked the door behind her. She refused to run in heels, no matter how irritated Dale was with her. She caught sight of him through her gated front door and his wavy blonde hair and classically handsome face sort of soothed her frustration with him. No denying the man was a perfect ten. Looks-wise at least.

He distractedly grabbed at her hand as she came down the stairs. "Did you call the super about your doorbell? You know I hate yelling up to you like that. It makes me feel like a teenager."

"Not yet."

Dale rolled his eyes and tugged her down the block toward a waiting cab. "Then maybe it's time you just made me a key. So I wouldn't have to go through that whole embarrassing ordeal every time I come over." He tossed his hand back toward her brownstone as if her home wasn't even worth wasting words on.

"I can't afford that," Lucy said, without shame.

"To get your keys copied? Jesus, Lucy, it costs like 5 dollars."

"No, I mean I can't afford to take a cab." Lucy pointed toward the street. She made good enough money as a physical therapist, but NYC living was expensive and she had her school loans. She usually just took the train.

"Well, I guess I'll just cover it, Lucy. As usual."

She sighed at his clipped tone and planted her feet. She'd hoped they could have lasted a little longer, he was super hot. But recently Dale had gone from mildly, and persistently, annoying to being an out and out dick.

"I don't let people talk to me like that, Dale." She crossed her arms over her chest.

"We'll talk about this in the cab, Lucy. The meter is running."

The cab driver peeked his head out the window, a curious expression on his face.

"Nah," she said, shaking her head. "We don't have to talk about it at all. I'm not getting in the cab." She let her arms drop and rearranged her purse on her hip. Dale's eyes widened. Obviously he'd never been dumped before. "We're done here, Dale. I deserve to be with someone who's nice to me."

"Lucy!" he admonishingly exclaimed.

"I'm real tired of you saying my name that way, Dale." She turned and headed toward the train station. "I'll bring your stuff by your house in a few days."

She didn't have to turn around to imagine the irate expression on his face.

"What are you looking at?" she heard him screech at the cabbie as he slammed the door.

Lucy felt a dull twinge as she heard the cab pull away, but she had to admit that she wasn't very bummed to have Dale out of her life. He wasn't ever anything more than a warm body to her. And recently, he hadn't been worth the trouble. She sighed and waited for the crosswalk light to change. Same old story, new day. All the dudes she'd dated in the last few years had all seemed so special at the beginning, and had all ended up either boring, or just plain assholes. She needed a change. A big one.

CHAPTER TWO

"Dude," the Oracle said to Amos through a mouthful of popcorn. "Chill out."

Through the TV screen, the two of them watched Lucy hurry gracefully down the stairs of the subway station. The King slept in his chambers behind them, but the Oracle had called up the images on the television screen so that Amos could supervise Lucy's capture. Nothing could go wrong.

"What?" Amos asked distractedly. He'd been trying to pretend the Oracle wasn't there, difficult with all the loud popcorn chewing.

The Oracle gestured to Amos's hands and looking down Amos saw that his dragon claws had unsheathed. God, what the hell was wrong with him? He'd been in control of his shifting since he was ten years old. He snicked the claws back in, his human fingers appearing. Why was he getting so worked up watching Lucy interact with that dumbass piece of human garbage?

Amos took a deep breath and ignored the Oracle's gaze on the side of his face. He just didn't like to see a woman get treated badly, that was all. He'd been strangely proud of Lucy when she'd severed ties with that loser. Which didn't make sense considering he hardly knew her. It also didn't make sense how unholy pissed he'd gotten when he'd realized that the dumbass was escorting her that night because he was her mate.

Well, not her mate anymore, he thought and a thrill shot through him. She'd, what did humans call it? Kicked his ass to the curb. But the feeling rising through him extinguished as he remembered who her new mate was going to be. The King. Amos glanced behind him at the King's locked chambers.

Concentrate, Mos. He thought to himself angrily. He hated this newfound wandering brain he was battling with. His whole life he'd been single minded in his pursuit of one thing –protect the royal line. Just like his father and grandfather and his father and on. He came from an endless line of Protectors, the most loyal of all the dragon breeds. And the most fierce.

Even in the ancient stories, it had been his family who protected the royals. When he'd been a boy, he'd been assigned to safeguard the young prince, along with an adult bodyguard, of course. But that had been the cushiest assignment that bodyguard had ever had, because nothing had gotten past Amos. More than eating, more than sleeping, or playing, or laughing, he'd been compelled to protect the prince. Just like he was compelled to protect the King now. There was nothing he wouldn't do to maintain his post as the King's personal bodyguard. He remembered the few years he'd spent as a teenager without a job assignment. It was after the young prince had fallen to the royal sickness. Amos had watched helplessly as the emaciated boy got skinnier and skinnier. Amos had been by his side as his eyes had gone glassy with death. He'd been the one to carry his body to the graveyard. He'd laid the boy in the ground himself.

And then he'd spent the next four years with no one to guard. Out of his mind with boredom and a racing in his chest that told him he was always in the wrong place, not doing enough, slacking, slacking, slacking. At the end of those four years he'd been able to run a mile in 4 minutes and 30 seconds and could drag a Buick behind him. And that was just in his human form.

He'd been devastated when his father had been killed in the line of duty, protecting King Dalyer. His father had pushed the King from a boat seconds before the explosion that took his life. Amos would have gone his whole life living in limbo, without another assignment, if it meant not losing his father. But what happened had happened. And it meant that Amos was promoted. King Dalyer's personal bodyguard.

Protecting the King meant something different everyday. Some days he shadowed him through the streets of the Kingdom, eyeing strangers suspiciously and ushering him into safe zones as fast as he could. Some days it meant tossing out food that didn't't smell quite right. And today it meant making sure that that woman made it through the portal safely. That gorgeous woman. That gorgeous woman with an ass that could make a man forget his own name.

"For fuck sake," he snapped at the Oracle when Amos realized that the reason he was staring at the woman's ass was because the Oracle had zoomed in on it. "Act like a professional."

"When have I ever claimed to be a professional?" the Oracle asked, popcorn stuck in his beard. "She's cute, this is boring, and we've gotta pass the time somehow."

"We're kidnapping this woman -to a different universe no less- to get her pregnant with another species by someone she's never met." Amos wasn't sure why he was yelling. "The least we can do is allow her a little dignity, here."

"Alright, alright, big guy." The Oracle raised his hands palm up. "Take a breather." The image zoomed out as she got off the train at her station and jogged up the stairs to street level. "Looks like the action is starting anyway."

It was. Amos clenched his jaw as two of the King's soldiers approached her in their human forms. Seeing two men walking swiftly toward her, Lucy darted to the other side of the street, hurrying now to get closer to the museum. She was smart and fast. She disappeared in the shadow of a building and the two soldiers ran to catch up with her, no longer trying to be stealthy.

For one confusingly hopeful moment, Amos thought she might get away. She shouldn't have to come here as a prisoner and be forced to breed. But the other part of him knew that the moment she was caught and dragged through the portal she'd be there in front of him. Living and warm and real. Not just an image on a screen anymore. He cleared his throat and adjusted his cock in his pants.

Control. Control. Control. He chanted to himself. He had to be under control when she came into the dragon realm. He'd have to wake the King and get down to the portal to receive her in a matter of minutes. But for now, heart in his throat, he watched the two soldiers catch up to Lucy. The men flanked her on either side and dragged her, screaming and fighting, into the night.

CHAPTER THREE

Lucy had always wondered how far she would go to protect herself. What she'd do to stay alive. As the two humongous men on either side of her kicked open a chained, wooden door and dragged her down an abandoned set of subway stairs, she finally had the answer to that question. The first chance she got, she was gonna murder these two shit heads.

She took advantage of their precarious footing on the stairs and lifted her feet, swinging her weight to the side. Catching the one on the left directly in the gut, he grunted as the three of them slipped down a few stairs. But they were too strong. They easily regained their footing and gripped even harder onto her arms.

"Comply with us," growled the other one in an accent she couldn't quite place. He pulled something shiny out of his coat. A syringe. "Or we'll be forced to subdue you."

Fearing whatever drug was in that syringe more than the bodily harm they were sure to inflict on her, Lucy went still.

She was desperate to know where they were taking her, but she refused to ask. She took a deep breath and tried to observe every detail about both of the men that she could. She'd want to tell the police anything that could help them track down these assholes as soon as she got away. Because she was getting away. There was no way she was dying in an abandoned subway station.

She observed them from the corners of her eyes. Plain black clothing, matching buzz cuts. They both wore diamond studs in their ears. Weird.

She craned her neck to catch sight of their faces, but it was too dark in the abandoned subway tunnel. Suddenly, they stopped, in complete unison with one another. The tunnel was so dark that Lucy couldn't see the end of her own nose. But in the darkness something glinted, like moonlight over a lake.

"On the count of three?" one asked and the other one shook his head, checking his phone.

"They're ready immediately."

"Wait, what? NO!" Lucy screamed as the two men lifted her clear off the ground and tossed her into thin air.

She was nowhere. She was nobody. There was only blackness, expansion, compression. She was growing and shrinking at the same time. Maybe this was death.

But then she had arms again, she felt them around her own ribcage. And she had legs, she could feel those too. She felt something strong and warm against her. Heard a heartbeat against her ear. Felt the solid step-step-step of someone who knew where they were going. Something smelled good. Like freshly dug earth and baking bread.

She opened her eyes and they ached all the way to the back of her head. She blinked the blur out of her eyes and realized she was cradled in someone's arms. Someone's gigantic arms. Like serious python arms. She tilted her head back and saw a black t shirt, the bottom of a sharp jaw, a buzzed head, and just a glimpse of a diamond earring...

Lucy lost her shit. With a war cry that would have made Xena proud, she scratched out at her kidnapper, catching him on the neck. Kicking her legs wildly, she beat her fists against him as hard as she could. After a few furious seconds she realized he hadn't even broken stride. She felt like a toddler throwing a tantrum, dwarfed by his size and manner. She turned her face toward his chest. Well, let's see if he could ignore this.

CHAPTER FOUR

Amos held Lucy a little further from his body as she kicked and punched and screamed. He couldn't take her warm body writhing around against him. Her dress was even thinner than it had looked on the television screen and as she threw herself around, it was working its way up her thighs. He refused to look down.

The minute he locked her in her chambers, he was gonna have to take a private moment for himself.

She sagged for a second. He hoped she'd tired herself out. King Dalyer would not think this was cute.

Amos, on the other hand, definitely thought it was a little cute. Watching her try to get out of his hold was like watching a kitten try to fight a black bear. She was just so fragile and little. So delicate like a-

"Fuck! Did you just bite me?" Amos was caught completely by surprise and bobbled her, losing his grip.

Taking her opportunity, Lucy slid down his body, stomped his foot with her high heel, and took off running.

Amos pressed his hand to his chest, checking to see if she'd drawn blood. Damn. That had hurt! So why the fuck was he at half mast? Shaking his head at himself, he figured she had enough of a head start. She was about 200 feet away from him at this point. Coming up fast on the fortress doors.

He beat her there and lazily leaned his back on the gate. She pulled up short, realizing he had cut her off and looked around wildly for another exit.

"This is the only way out," he said.

Her ice blue eyes snapped to his and he felt it like an electric shock straight to his groin.

"That's what you'd say no matter if it were true or not," she snapped.

He shrugged. Pretended that hearing the husk her voice had taken on from screaming didn't affect him.

"Of course."

"Soooo. In that case," she said and turned to sprint in the other direction.

She'd gotten approximately four steps before he was standing in her path again. His feet planted and his arms crossed. She turned yet again but this time his arm darted out and gently looped her waist. She tried to scratch him again so he grabbed her by the wrists and whipped her arms up over her head. She tugged away from him and it drew her very full breasts up and almost out the top of her dress.

He dragged his eyes up to her parted lips. He licked his own, felt himself pulling her a little closer. But when he looked up at her brilliant blue eyes, he saw fear in them. Mortal fear.

He sighed. "What if I promised I would never hurt you."

She glared up at him, anger joining the fear in her eyes. "Stop lying to me."

"I'm not lying. I'm promising."

She stopped tugging and looked up at him, thoroughly confused.

He thought of how important she was to the King. How much the royal line completely and utterly depended on her.

"What if I swore that I would never let harm come to you. That I'd die for you if it came to it."

He felt the air change between them and knew that the rawest of the fear was leaving her. It was replaced with racing thoughts, a desperation to understand what the hell was going on.

He continued on. "If you can accept that promise then I can start explaining where you are why you're here."

"And you'll let go of me?" she asked, her eyes big and gentle and, God, was she weepy? Shit. He really didn't't want to see her cry.

"I'll let go of you," he agreed.

"Ok. Then in that case, I believe you won't hurt me. I accept your promise."

He held on to her for another second. Just the briefest of moments. He didn't want to let go of her. He wanted to touch her more. He wanted to see if the skin on her neck was as soft as the skin on her wrists. He wanted to lift her up again the way he'd carried her from the portal. With her pressed so firmly into him. Her beautiful face against his chest. He wanted to have a reason to keep on holding her. But he didn't have a reason. She wasn't his to touch or hold. She was the King Dalyer's. From the moment the Oracle had tracked her down in the human realm, she had become King Dalyer's most important possession.

Amos's stomach curdled slightly at the thought. He settled for swiping his thumb across one of her wrists, just once. Committing the feeling to memory.

The second he loosened his grip she yanked herself away from him. Growling, he chased after her, tiring of the game.

"What the fuck, little hatchling." He growled deep in his chest and snared her wrists again. "Quit doing that."

She yanked at him. "Well, promising not to hurt me pretty much makes it a no brainer for me to keep trying to escape." Her eyes sparked with an internal fire and he realized that she had never been close to crying before. She'd been playing him. And he'd let himself be played.

This was ridiculous. He was one of the fiercest warriors in the entire dragon realm. The freaking KING trusted him above all other people. And here he was unable to get this tiny little human from one room to the next.   Fed up, he bent down and tossed her over his shoulder. He strode across the great hallway and toward the King's chambers. Amos was careful to hold her in such a way that she couldn't bite him again.

"Hey!" she screeched. "You said you wouldn't hurt me!"

"Am I hurting you?"

Her staunch, irritated silence told him that he wasn't.

"I didn't promise not to restrain you. And actually I'm keeping my promise by not letting you escape from the fortress. It's not safe out there for you, hatchling."

CHAPTER FIVE

"Fortress?" She immediately stiffened in his arms. Looking around at the windowless hallway, the dingy gray stone walls, the lanterns burning every few feet, her eyes grew wide. "What the hell is this place? Oh my God. This is one of those BDSM dungeons isn't it."

Apparently deciding that she was done fighting him, he flipped her off his shoulder so he could carry her in front of him again. He looked down at her as he walked.

"What's BSDM?" he asked.

Lucy instantly felt her cheeks set on fire. She had never been in a weirder situation. "It's like, um, you know. When people tie each other up and like, have pain sex?"

"Pain sex?" His brow furrowed.

She was suddenly very aware of her breasts that were sort of crushing into his chest. For some reason, she couldn't seem to look him in the face. "You know, like the whole pleasure/pain thing."

"Pleasure/pain," he repeated, completely deadpan.

"Yeah, like, hurts so good? That kinda thing?"

"This is the kind of sex you have?" His voice had grown very deep. Lucy could feel it vibrate out from his chest and through her. She was suddenly very hot.

"No, no. I mean not really. Not formally. But, like, who hasn't been spanked every now and then."

He grunted a little and she darted her eyes up to his face. He stared down at her, his eyes dark and hooded. And really, really brown. Like crazy, amber-ish, gorgeous brown.

"Spanked," he repeated.

Lucy scrubbed her hands through the air. "You know what, this is so

not the point. Would you just tell me where the hell I am?"

"We're here now. So, I guess the King will tell you."

"King?!" Lucy had heard enough. Twenty minutes ago she'd been on her way to an art show in Queens. And since then she'd been accosted on the street, dragged into a dirty, abandoned subway tunnel, tossed into some sort of black hole, manhandled, chased around, and manhandled some more.

"Sure, why not." She threw her hands in the air. "Of course there's a King."

Muscle man set her down in front of two incredibly ornate stone doors. Giant creatures were carved in great, curling patterns. Gems sparkled in their eyes.

"You'll be reverent with the King, hatchling." he said to her, one hand still on her shoulder. "He won't be happy otherwise."

She looked up at him, a retort on her tongue, but it died when she saw his genuine expression. He was worried about her.

She shrugged. "Fine. As long as I get some answers."

"You'll get answers." He went to push open the door but paused and turned back to her. "Just, maybe don't mention pain sex to him."

"Oh my God." Lucy face palmed. "I am not usually out here just talking about BDSM. I'm flustered, ok!"

"Ok," he said, his voice low and his eyes dark. In a move that completely surprised her, he reached out like he was gonna touch her face, but dropped his hand. "Just remember my promise to you."

This whole situation was thoroughly fucked up and the first chance she got, Lucy knew she was getting the hell out of here. But for some reason, she believed him. She believed he was going to protect her. No matter what.

"Let's meet the King."

This King Dalyer certainly had a very specific... style. Lucy thought as she looked around the huge chamber. Again, no windows, but plenty of gold filigree, embedded gems, and an absolutely ridiculous amount of velvet. Seriously, how many skeins of velvet had to die to outfit all the drapes in this joint.

The King sat straight in a comically large throne. It was ten times taller and wider than it had to be. The King sat in the middle of it, making him look like he'd been shrunk down. So weird. Actually, now that she thought about it, everything was gigantic. Even the lanterns on the wall were the size of refrigerators.

The King had yet to speak. So far he'd just stared at her with disturbingly dark eyes. Like a snake's.

Lucy refused to fidget under his gaze, but it had been a fairly stressful evening and no one had offered to show her to the bathroom. Just as she was about to ask for one, the King spoke.

"You're healthy?" he asked.

Kind of flummoxed, Lucy turned to Muscle Man for clarification. He tossed his head toward the King like, answer.

She turned back. "Yeah. I am."

She wondered if maybe she should have lied. Told him she had some sort of disgusting disease so that he'd let her go.

"But you have Ellington's syndrome."

Lucy gaped at him. How the hell did he know that? It wasn't a deadly disease or anything, just a chromosomal disorder that changed the way she processed proteins. Most people went their whole lives without even knowing they had it. "You accessed my medical records?"

He didn't answer her question. Instead asked another one. "And your mother had asthma, yes? A very particular form?"

Lucy out and out refused to answer this question. She was not about to discuss her mother with this creepy ass man in a weirdly big chair. But Muscles nudged her. She needed to answer.

She nodded curtly.

A smile curled into King Dalyer's face and Lucy fought not to shiver against it. It made him even creepier.

"Why, you're a miracle." The King's voice had a quiet, fascinated edge to it. "Almost as if you were designed just for me."

Lucy's blood froze. Tonight she'd been frustrated, angry, startled, nervous, confused, and very scared. But this was the first time she was truly frightened. She felt sick imagining what he meant by that. She shuffled her feet just slightly and immediately felt the warmth of Muscles beside her. Apparently her body had decided it was time to move a little closer to him.

"You see, my family has had a little problem over the last few generations." The King still hadn't moved an inch in the chair and his unnatural stillness disturbed her. "Most of our children die."

At that, he lifted one hand and examined one of the many rings on his fingers. "Even those who make it to adulthood are... weaker than the ancestors. Soon we won't even be able to defend the throne. Especially from this pesky little rebel alliance that keeps rearing its head."

"Defend the throne with just physical strength?" Lucy asked, unable to keep from cutting in. "Isn't that a little medieval? Couldn't you try, I don't know, negotiations?"

The King stared at Lucy incredulously, letting out a low chuckle. Even Muscles gave a little chuff of surprise from next to her.

"Child, that is not our way. We are creatures of battle."

Lucy shrugged, kind of odd phrasing, but whatever. "Alright. So what do I have to do with any of this?" She was one second away from stomping her foot.

"You," the King said as he finally broke his stick-straight posture and leaned forward, studying her. "Are a delightful little cocktail of DNA. And any child of mine, borne by you, would be the most powerful being in the land."

Lucy's jaw dropped. What. The. Royal. Fuck.

CHAPTER SIX

Amos tried hard not to grimace at the look on Lucy's face. She was looking at the King like he was an absolute psycho. King Dalyer was not going to put up with that for long until he took offense and punished her insolence.

Perhaps thinking that she didn't understand what he'd said, the King went on. "We will mate. You will bear me offspring that will be the heir to this throne."

With that, Lucy's mouth clapped shut. She brought one hand up and rubbed across her forehead, like she had a headache. Crossing her arms over her ample chest, she looked up at the King.

"Yeah. I'm gonna take a pass. Hard pass."

"Excuse me, human?" The King's eyes glittered like stones at the bottom of a well. Amos knew what was coming, even if Lucy had no earthly clue. He took one step in front of her, not blocking her, just getting ready.

"What makes you think you have a choice in the matter?" The King's voice dropped to a level so deep it bounced off the walls like bass. "It's laughable to think you are even capable of refusing me. You're powerless here, human."

Amos heard Lucy gasp behind him as the King tossed his head backwards and his long, suddenly reptilian tongue lashed out at the air. Bone spikes shot out of his spine and his skin took on a blood red hue as scales unshackled and clicked themselves into place. His tail curled around him and landed with a wet thump on the floor. He shot upwards and outwards, tripling in size in the blink of an eye. With a sharp sound, his claws clicked out and there he sat on the throne, full dragon.

Amos could hear Lucy's panicked breath, but could also feel King Dalyer's rage directed toward her. Something in him told him to shift to his dragon form as well. But never once had he shifted to face off with the King. It made him sick to think about it. But he had to de-escalate the situation. If the King hurt Lucy, it could forever doom the royal line.

"Your highness, she's not safe here right now." He stepped fully in front of her. "I'm taking her away. We can finish this later."

The King must have seen the logic in what Amos said because the blood red dragon leaned back in the throne. He raised a monstrous, clawed paw and dismissed them.

"Go," Amos whispered to Lucy. She didn't need telling twice as she scrambled out of the throne room and into the cold stone hallway.

"Amos," the King's voice stopped him at the threshold. "Make sure she doesn't attempt to escape tonight. She'll injure herself if she does."

Amos nodded. "I'll assign Rodrigo to watch her."

"No," the King said. "Rodrigo will take me tonight. You will stay with her."

It was not in Amos's training to argue with King Dalyer. He gave a curt nod of assent. He shot a quick text to Rodrigo. He was professional and a fierce fighter. The King would be fine for the night. He turned and followed Lucy out of the hall, slamming the chamber doors closed behind them.

"Shit," Amos said as he assessed her. She was white as milk and her eyes were dilated. She was completely panicking. He had to get her to her chambers and calm her down.

He reached out to comfort her, or pick her up, or hug her, he didn't know. But she swatted his hand away, leaning heavily on the wall. He swatted her hands away in return and took her face in both hands, examining her eyes, feeling her sweaty brow. Again, his eyes dropped to her lips. They were fuller than he was used to, plump. He bit down on the urge to pull her closer and closer. Touch those lips to any part of his body. He didn't even care.

"Well, I guess now I understand why the throne is so big." Her voice was surprisingly steady.

Amos nodded and let his hands drop to his sides. "Most of the fortress is designed to accommodate us in both human and dragon forms."

Lucy glanced up at him suspiciously. And pressed herself a little further away. He realized that she hadn't guessed that he was a shifter too. She'd thought it was just the King.

"You need water," Amos said and tugged her away from the wall, ignoring the way she tried to shrink from his touch. Looking back and studying her blanched face he continued. "And meat. And wine. And whiskey. And sleep."

"What, you want me to puke all over you?" Lucy asked, stumbling along as his pace quickened even further.

Amos turned a corner and immediately halted in his tracks. Lucy kept walking and smashed into him. He felt the imprint of her body on his and felt a flame of lust erupt inside of him. As soon as he locked her in her chambers he was going to shift. Full dragon. And he was going to fly at least 100 miles. And when he shifted back to his human form, he was going to the city to find some shifter wench. It had obviously been too long since he'd gotten some action.

He pushed aside a floor length velvet tapestry to reveal another intricate carving in the heavy stone. He pressed the ruby eye of one of the two carved dragons. The door to her chamber swung open and without hesitating he shoved Lucy into the small room. She stumbled on her heels but he didn't care, he just had to get out of there before he did something dumb.

Then her words registered.

"Puke?" he asked, pausing at the door. "Why would you puke?"

Lucy turned a circle, taking in her room. "Because eating meat and then drinking wine and whiskey would make me puke. It's gross. Can't I get, like, some pad thai or something?"

"No, we don't have pad thai here."

Lucy eyed him shrewdly. "So that must mean we're not in a city. If you can't order thai food. Are we out in the 'burbs somewhere?"

"No, Lucy. We're not on earth." He spoke slowly and clearly, gently closing the door behind him. She needed to hear the truth.

She slowly sat down on the bed, bouncing slightly. Amos's mouth watered as her dress snuck up her thigh again.

"Not on earth," she repeated dully. "Well, I guess I shouldn't be surprised considering I just watched a Mr. Burns look-alike transform into a bright red dragon."

Amos shook his head and didn't ask what she was talking about.

Her face lit with sudden understanding. "That sparkling black hole thing. In the subway tunnel."

Amos confirmed. "The portal. Between the human realm and the dragon realm."

"Those men tossed me through it."

"And I caught you on the other side." Amos thought about the moment her unconscious form had fallen gently through the portal. He thought of her weight in his arms, the first moment he'd felt her warmth. And the raging erection he'd immediately gotten.

"How are you so calm about this, hatchling?" He had to know.

"No choice, I guess," she responded. "I'll figure a way out of all of this. I always do."

Amos understood what she was saying but it made his stomach drop. She still believed she had the option of a different fate. He had to get her to understand. "The King usually gets what he wants, hatchling."

"This is too much." She flopped backwards on the bed, arms outspread and Amos jammed his hands in his pockets. Let his eyes rove hungrily across her curvy body. Let himself look all he wanted, considering she was staring at the ceiling. She sat halfway up and he averted his eyes. "You're right," she said. "I need water. And food. And sleep." She stood up abruptly. "And to pee."

Amos raised his eyebrows at her and gestured toward a small room off of her chambers.

She closed the door behind her and Amos sat down in her place on the bed. Felt the warmth her body had left behind.

"Are we alone in the fortress?" she called out from behind the closed bathroom door.

For a second Amos thought she meant just the two of them. But she continued on. "Shouldn't there be servants, or courtiers, or something?" She opened the bathroom door, wiping her hands on a hand towel that she tossed back toward the sink.
Crossing the room back toward Amos, she toed out of one high heel then the other.

Amos cleared his throat and stood up to fill a goblet of water for her. Handing it over, he sat next to her on the bed, his weight creating a valley she couldn't help but slip into.

"Just the King and I are allowed to know you're here. The men who captured you have no idea... what you're for. We've forbidden anyone from this part of the fortress for now. And it's impossible for anyone to enter without me knowing. Or for anyone to exit." His eyes narrowed meaningfully.

"Don't worry. I'm too tired to try and escape tonight." He almost believed her.

She looked him up and down. "Why all the security to keep me a big secret?"

"Because no one can know about you. Ever." He found he had trouble looking in her face as he told her the shameful truth.

"Because then it might get out that the King and his offspring are weak?" she asked.

Amos nodded. "Yes. But also," he paused. "Dragon shifters don't breed with humans. It's taboo."

Lucy cocked her head to one side. "Let me guess. Dragon shifters think humans are disgusting?"

"No," he shook his head. "Not disgusting. Just... less."

Lucy nodded and ran a hand through her long hair. It had gotten messy through all the events of the evening, but Amos found he liked it that way.

"In a weird way, I kind of get that," she said. "I mean, in terms of supernatural stuff I offer zilch. I'm not even good at sports. All I can do is jog." She grinned at him and he felt completely disabled. As if she'd just stabbed him in the stomach.

God, she was so beautiful. Disturbingly beautiful. Inconveniently beautiful. Disastrously beautiful.

"And it was pretty impressive," she continued. "Watching the King hulk out like that."

She put her water on the ground and turned to face him, crossing her legs on the bed. "Can you do that?"

"Shift?"

She nodded. "As fast as that?"

Amos scoffed. "Much faster than that." He snapped his fingers to show just how fast.

"Can I see your dragon?"

The question was asked innocently enough but Amos found he had to shift his elbows onto his knees to hide his enormous erection. It was already too much having her warm and smelling so good and sitting so close. But now she wanted to see his dragon form. God.

He shook his head.

"Why not?"

He gestured around to her chambers, spacious enough for a human, he supposed. The King had made sure she'd be comfortable there. "I wouldn't fit."

Lucy's eyes widened as she looked around her. "The King would fit in here in dragon form. Easily."

He looked down at her. "I'm bigger than the King. Much bigger."

Amos realized that her eyes had dropped to his lips. And, fuck, was she leaning toward him? He froze.

Her ice blue eyes went back up to his. "Can you show me just a little? Like, shift just a little bit?"

"Fuck," Amos said. He was so screwed. He was going to do it. Anything she asked.

She smiled. She knew she was getting what she wanted.   Not breaking eye contact with her, Amos allowed his eyes to shift. He knew the pupils would turn to slits, they'd go iridescent, like a cat's.

Lucy gasped and leaned in for a closer look. "More," she whispered.

Thinking of what other minor shift he could do, Amos held one of his arms out in between them and let his scales cover it. They were a glittering amber green in the flickering candlelight.

Lucy's eyes widened as she leaned even closer to him. "More."

Well, she asked for it.

Her breath went out in an amazed whoosh as he let his wings unfurl behind him. He could barely open them halfway in this confining room.

"Oh my gosh." Her eyes filled with tears but he knew she wasn't scared.

She reached out to touch his scales but he immediately sheathed them. Her hand landed on the human skin of his arm.

"The scales are sharp," he explained, his voice gruff. She hadn't moved her hand from his arm. She trailed it up to his shoulder.

"You're beautiful," she said.

He blinked his eyes roughly and when he opened them, they were human again. His wings folded up and disappeared. He was to his full human form again. "Not beautiful. Fierce. Scary."

"Very beautiful," she disagreed.

"You're very beautiful," he said, before he could stop himself. Her face was so close to his and he was hyperaware of her hand on his shoulder.

"Nah," she said, her eyes searching his. "I get 'cute' a lot. In a chubby way. But not beautiful."

His brain fogged over in angry confusion. "You're not chubby. You're a woman. With all the stuff a woman is supposed to have." He gestured to her chest and ass. He quickly dropped his hand. This was not going as planned.

She cocked her head to one side and finally let her hand fall away from his shoulder.

"That's not the general consensus. Most people.."

He cut her off by grabbing her hand and placing it back on his shoulder. He didn't want her to keep talking like that. He took her other hand and brought it around her back so she wouldn't get any more ideas of touching him elsewhere. He would snap if she did that. But their fingers tangled behind her back. He allowed himself that much.

"Most people are fucking idiots," he said gruffly. "I'm not most people. And I say you're fucking gorgeous."

She let out a loud breath, just a kiss away from being a moan. She licked her lips. He pretty much wanted to fuck her mouth with his mouth.

He mentally shook himself. Control, control, control.

She was not his to touch. She was the King's. She wiggled a little in his grasp, like she wanted to get closer to him. And he couldn't close himself off completely.

He leaned into her neck and deeply inhaled her scent. It was warm and made his mouth water, something he couldn't quite place.

"So goddamn hot, I've been hard since you came through the portal."

CHAPTER SEVEN

Lucy looked down and gaped. Wow, he wasn't lying. That gigantic bulge was promising. Very promising. She licked her lips.

Considering how much stress she under, she was pretty surprised at how wet she'd gotten from being alone with him. But there was no denying the warmth moving down her thighs. She pressed them together against the ache and his eyes tracked the movement.

Alright. Game time. She tried to tug her hand from where he had it pinned behind her back, but he held it fast.

She struggled a little more and his eyes darted to hers. This time she really yanked her arm but he just clamped her against him, pinning her. Her nipples pulled tight and beaded against the lace of her bra as she quickly shifted her legs so that they circled his waist. Her dress strained around her open thighs.

His nostrils flared as she watched him. A feral lust flashed across his face and something deep inside of her clenched. She started to bring her mouth to his but he held her away.

"We can't do that." His voice was clipped and strained.

She tried to kiss him again, squeezing her legs around his waist and drawing his face with her free hand. His eyes closed and she could taste his breath on her lips. But again, he jerked his face away. This time he grabbed both of her wrists in one hand and held them up over her head.

"Hatchling..." he growled.

She quickly shifted her weight and took him by surprise, toppling them backwards. She leaned in again but he deftly rolled them over so that she was on her back, legs around his waist and arms pinned above her head. She felt her breasts press against the top of her dress. She glanced down to see if they'd popped out and he followed her gaze down.

"Fuck," he swore, dropping his head to her shoulder. "You are so unbelievably sexy." He lifted his head and looked down at her.

"We can't do this," he said again, but his hips thrust slightly forward, His bulge rubbing firmly against her wet, aching center.

"Fuck," she said, dropping her head back and grinding herself against him. "We can definitely do this."

He thrust against her again and groaned. She bit her lip and met him. If he kept going just like that, she would come apart in about T minus 10 seconds.

But he stopped. He rested his forehead on hers. She realized that his eyes were the same clear green-brown of his scales. She pressed herself against him again, and something hot and dangerous flashed across his face, but he didn't move.

He reached back and unwound her legs from his waist. Letting her arms free, he took a quick step back from the bed.

They stared one another down. Breathing hard. She felt tears of frustration form. She'd been through the ringer tonight and little bit of release could have really helped relieve some tension. And here he was,

Mr. Wet Blanket. Mr. Ungodly Muscle Bound Wet Blanket. Well, she wasn't done.

Jumping down from the bed, she walked over to him and turned her back. "It's been a long day and I'm going to bed. Help me with my dress?"

She swept her hair to one side, revealing the zipper. It was a move she'd used many times. If dragon shifters were anything like human men, he'd be begging to touch her in about three minutes.

She felt his stiff exhale wash over her back and then a gentle tug at the top of her dress. She rolled her eyes when she realized he was doing everything he could to not actually touch her. She glanced back over her shoulder at him, shooting him a coquettish look. "All the way down, please."

He cleared his throat and did not look up from his task. Slowly her dress unzipped. Lucy held it up across her breasts so it wouldn't fall. She felt his last tug and realized it was fully open. She turned to face him and let the dress fall.

CHAPTER EIGHT

Just kill me now. Seriously. Death was an easier choice than the one he had in front of him. Why did her underwear have to be black. And see-through. He had a thing for black see-through underwear.

The flimsy excuse for a bra barely contained her incredibly full breasts. Her nipples pressed toward him and he could see they were the same dark pink of her mouth. Her soft stomach curved in at the waist and flared immediately back out at her hips and ass. The tiny triangle of underwear covering her pussy was obviously soaked through with her need.

"Now I'm cold," she said, crossing her arms under her breasts and pushing them up even further. They strained against the lingerie. "Come warm me up."

"I can't touch you like that," he snapped. His voice was louder and colder than he'd intended, but he was hanging on by a thread.

She glared at him accusingly. "You promised you wouldn't hurt me. But this is hurting me."

He threw his hands up. "Oh for fuck sake. I didn't mean emotional pain." He felt like a dick for even having to say that out loud.

"It's physical pain," she said. Her eyes were hooded. Her cheeks kissed with color. A piece of her jet black hair fell lovingly over her shoulder and caressed one of the raspberry nipples that were peeking at him through the dark lace bra.

"It hurts here," she said.

His life both ended and began as she pressed one of her hands to her pussy.

Something in Amos broke. Like a boat's tether in a hurricane. He wasn't the same man he was when he entered that room. But he couldn't touch her. Everything he stood for, everything that he was born to honor would be betrayed if he touched her. But somehow, turning from her felt like an even bigger betrayal.

He made a snap decision. He quickly grabbed an armchair that sat in the corner and set it down where he'd been standing. He sat down and folded his hands in front of him. He felt like he'd spent the last few hours trying to stop looking at her. But now, there was nothing stopping him. He cleared his throat and leaned back.

"That hand between your legs, that's my hand. You understand?" His voice was low and deadly.

She immediately nodded.

"Whatever I want to do with that hand, I get to do."

She nodded again, a blush rising alluringly on her body.

"Turn around."

He barely stifled a groan when he realized she was wearing a thong. Had been wearing a thong the entire night. Wearing a thong when he'd carried her in his arms. Wearing a thong when she was sprinting toward the gate, Wearing a thong when he'd tossed her over his shoulder and only her dress had separated his face from her soft, curvy ass. He adjusted his cock against his pants, she wasn't the only one this was painful for.

"Good. Now take down your underwear. Slowly." There wasn't much more of her body to even be revealed at this point, but Amos couldn't tear his eyes away from where her underwear had been. She bent forward to take them the rest of the way down and Amos got a front row seat to her perfect little pussy from behind.

This was actually gonna kill him. His heart pounded out of his chest and he clamped his hands to the arms of the chair.

"No," he said as she moved to stand back up. "Stay bent. Let me look at you." He could have looked for an hour, but she wiggled just a tiny bit and he knew she was getting needy.

"The bra," he bit out. "Face me."

Lucy instantly stripped off her bra and turned around. And there were no words. She wasn't just hot. This was the most attractive woman he'd ever seen. He couldn't have dreamed her up if he'd tried. Wouldn't have believed someone if they'd described her. Each curve was so extreme, so soft and feminine. She was made to be naked.

"Clothes are a crime against humanity," he murmured.

She shifted on her feet. She was as ready as he was.

"Sit on the bed and spread your legs."

In complete control of the sexiest situation of his life, he and his cock were currently best friends and mortal enemies. As he watched her, he had to stroke himself, at least once.

Her eyes followed the movement of his hand over his pants and she licked her lips.

"I could help you with that," she said in a voice husky with lust.

He shook his head. "No. That's not what you're gonna do." He leaned forward in the chair, his own stupid fucking code of honor the only thing keeping him there. "What you're gonna do, is fuck that hand."

Her eyes dilated and he knew she liked that plan.

"First, I want you to show me how wet you are." He could barely get the words out. "I want to see those fingers disappear inside you."

A bomb could have gone off in the room and he still wouldn't have been able to look away from Lucy's fingers as they came between her spread legs. Gently she parted herself and he could see just how wet and ready she was. For him. He leaned forward even further in his chair, like his body was trying to make his brain do what it wanted. What it needed.

He felt her gaze on his face but he couldn't look away from her pussy. He was rewarded when her middle finger sank into her wetness.

"Oh, god." Her back arched off the bed and he realized that she was so close it wasn't going to take much to put her over the edge.

She slid her ring finger in to join the first and she moaned, her head thrashing from one side to the other.

"Do it, Lucy," he growled.

She followed directions. She held her hand still but started to work her hips up and down on it. Suddenly she propped herself up on her other arm to give herself some purchase. She really started to ride the hand between her legs. Her head fell back on a moan. He watched in fascination as she brushed her thumb across her clit, once, twice.

Her body began to tense.

"Tell me if you're going to come," he snarled.

"I'm gonna come," she said instantly.

And if he thought he'd gone off the deep end before, he truly lost it now. His body would not let him stay in the chair. Something about her was calling out to him, screaming out for him. It was in her scent, her moans, the way she looked in the candlelight.

Something old and buried deep was waking up in Amos. Something he'd never known was in him was calling out to her too. It was turning him into an animal. It was the way he felt when he was in dragon form. It was screaming for him to be there when she came. To touch her into it. He suddenly knew, in his bones, that it would go against the laws of nature for her orgasm to disappear into the air.

He needed to swallow it. To make it his and only his. That orgasm belonged to him.

Up from his chair in a flash, he gently batted her hand away from herself. He barely registered her surprise as he grabbed her by the ankles and yanked her down the bed toward him. He knelt down in between her legs. And stared her in the eyes as he lowered his mouth to her.

CHAPTER NINE

Lucy awoke with a start. She was completely naked and covered over in a −surprise surprise- heavy velvet blanket. She wasn't confused or disoriented. She was in the fucking dragon fortress.

She was a little surprised to be alone though. Last she thing she knew the hottest, most talented mouth she'd ever experienced was bringing her to the most powerful orgasm of her life. Immediately afterward every bit of her energy had melted away. The fatigue, fear, and intensity of the day had caught up to her. And as he stroked the tension out of her body with his mouth, she'd fallen into a dark sleep.

She peered around the dim room. She wanted to call out for him but she realized she didn't even know his name.

"Oh my god," she lowered her face into her palm. Asking him was going to be extremely embarrassing.

"Miss?" a small voice came from the corner and startled the crap out of Lucy.

She tugged the sheet up to cover herself and tried to see through the darkness to whoever had spoken. "Who's there?"

"Me, Miss." A beautiful woman stepped out of the shadows. She had wavy brown hair to her waist and was wearing a simple blue dress. Her plain attire was starkly contrasted by an intricate gold choker across her neck.

She approached the bed and picked up a small oil lamp on the stand beside it. The light threw a forest of shadows across the bedroom. As it illuminated the woman's face, Lucy realized she was actually more of a girl. She couldn't be more than fifteen or sixteen.

"My name is Zara," she said and perched on the edge of the bed.

"I'm Lucy."

"Yes," Zara said with a small smile. "I know all about you."

"I thought I was supposed to be a big secret."

"Oh you are! But not from the wives. We've been informed of your importance."

Lucy had a sick feeling in her stomach. "Wives?"

"Yes," Zara nodded and nervously played with her choker. "I'm one of the King's three wives. Well, four now, if you count."

"I don't count," Lucy said firmly. And then, because she couldn't help herself, "How could you possibly be taken for a wife at your age. You're a child!"

Zara blushed and let her hair fall across her face. "I've been a wife to the King since I was born. But we haven't consummated yet. Dragon shifters can't conceive until they are at least twenty years of age. I'm only sixteen. My body won't accept him."

Lucy wasn't entirely sure what that meant but she was deeply relieved to hear it. "Thank god."

Zara nodded, but quickly stopped herself, as if she were embarrassed by her behavior.

Lucy glanced around the room again. "Uh, do you know where... Muscle Man is?"

Zara laughed in surprise. "You mean Amos? Your bodyguard?"

Amos. The name fit him. Lucy nodded.

"He's outside your door, Miss." She cleared her throat. "Guarding you."

So. He made her come so hard she met god. And then he went back to work. Interesting. Very interesting. Lucy wondered what he'd be like when she saw him next. Whether or not he was going to act like the whole thing hadn't happened. She decided not to dwell on it. She turned back to the girl.

"Zara, you've seen me naked. You can call me Lucy."

Zara laughed again and it was an unpracticed sound, almost like she wasn't used to feeling joy. Well, Lucy considered, if she'd been King Dalyer's wife since she was born, she probably hadn't led a very joyful life.

"It's time to get you ready to meet with the King, Mi- Lucy," Zara said and moved to the big wardrobe on one side of the room.

"I didn't realize I was meeting with the King today." Lucy's head hurt just thinking about it.

"Yes," Zara said as she perused through the many hanging gowns in the wardrobe. "He likes to see his wives every day. We'll all be there."

She pulled a simple green gown off the hanger and held it up, seeking Lucy's approval.

Lucy shrugged a yes at the dress. Foregoing modesty she tossed back the covers. "I'm gonna take a shower real quick."

"Okay," Zara said timidly.

Lucy stepped in to the wrought iron tub and fiddled with the taps. Liquid heaven poured out of a shower head shaped like a dragon's mouth. There was no curtain and looking up from the spray, she realized Zara was standing awkwardly in the middle of the bathroom

"You're not gonna, like, try to bathe me are you?" Lucy asked the girl.

"No! I'm not your servant, Miss. Lucy," she amended. "I'm your..."

"Friend?" Lucy said.

Zara blushed deeply and a pleased look came over her face.

She was a little awkward, but Lucy realized that she'd probably been deprived of affection for her whole life.

"Hand me that shampoo, will you?" Lucy asked and Zara brought some over to the shower. "Zara, if we're friends then can I ask you a question?"

Zara nodded and sat down on a small bench, listening so intently it kind of broke Lucy's heart. Poor lonely girl.

"When you saw Amos this morning, how'd he look?"

Zara looked a little confused by the question but she answered anyway. "The same as always. Serious. Well, maybe he was a little angrier than usual?"

"Angry how?"

"Well, he scowled at me. Usually he smiles."

Angry. Hmmm. Not quite sure what to make of that, Lucy finished washing her hair. She supposed she'd find out herself when they left her chambers to see the King.

Zara handed a towel to her and waited in the bedroom while Lucy dried off and studied herself in the mirror. For what a shitty day yesterday was, Lucy had to admit she looked pretty good. Glowy actually. A heart stopping, mind blowing orgasm would do that for a girl.

Zara had the green dress all unlaced and ready for Lucy when she came out of the steamy bathroom. She even had some weird undergarments picked out for her.

"What are those?" Lucy asked Zara.

Zara blushed. "The King likes for us to wear them. They protect our chastity for him."

Lucy leaned down and examined the shiny, intricately braided underwear.

"I'll bet they do. Jesus, it's made of metal!" Lucy cried, holding them up on the tip of her finger.

"Yes," Zara nodded. "And they lock onto you. Yours can only be unlocked with this key." She held a little black key up. "The wives keep the keys for one another. So no man besides the King can unlock them."

"Yeah," Lucy said as she tossed the garment back on the bed. "I'm gonna go ahead and go commando."

"Commando?" Zara asked, cocking her head to one side.

"No undies. Breeze between the knees."

Zara laughed and clapped a hand over her mouth. "But the King demands we wear them!"

"Does he ever check?"

"Well," Zara said and pulled uncomfortably at her choker. "I guess not."

"Ok, then I'm gonna pass." Lucy tossed them into the wardrobe where they fell with a little metallic jingle.

Zara looked like she wanted to say more, but instead she just held up the dress for Lucy to step into. They got the dress buttoned about half way up before they sagged against each other, panting.

"Yikes. Got anything a size up?" Lucy asked.

Zara sucked her lips in and tried to hold back a giggle. She shook her head. "They're all the same size."

"Oh my god!" Lucy exclaimed, eyeing herself in the gilded mirror on the wall. "I can't go out there like this. It looks like my boobs are eating me."

Both Zara and Lucy burst out laughing. Lucy was right, her breasts were bursting out the top of her dress, the fabric straining to accommodate her voluptuous figure. Suddenly the door to her chambers opened.

"Is everything alright?" Amos froze solid when he entered the room. He cleared his throat. "You're laughing. Sorry. I wasn't sure what the noise was."

He turned to leave but Lucy stepped toward him as if they were bound by some electric thread. "Wait, we need help."

He paused at the door but didn't look at her.

"We can't get my dress closed. We need someone strong."

Zara's eyes darted back and forth between Lucy and Amos. Zara was young, but she wasn't dumb, she took a step backwards and tried to fade in with the tapestries.

"That's ridiculous," Amos growled.

Lucy didn't back down. "I'm serious. We can't get this thing on. And unless you want me to go see the King looking like this..."

She gestured to her breasts that were basically falling out of her dress and she hadn't even finished speaking before Amos had come to stand behind her.

His fingers quickly did up button after button. He got to the buttons at the top, the ones her breasts were preventing from closing, and he firmly yanked the fabric. Lucy let out a little gasping breath as the dress constricted her. She felt Amos's breath feather over her neck and shoulders.

He was pretending to be cold to her, but Lucy could feel the heat between them. Every light scrape of his fingers against the smooth skin of her back sent waves of electricity between her legs. He finally did up the last button and the fabric strained around her chest, creating some of the most fantastic cleavage she'd ever had.

"Thank you, Amos," she whispered.

His eyes shot up to meet hers in the mirror when she said his name. Her mouth parted and she ran her tongue over her bottom lip. He cleared his throat and took a step back from her.

"The King is waiting," he said and strode out of the room.

So, he was going without acknowledging what happened last night. It bothered Lucy more than she wanted to admit. She was usually fine with a one-and-done. But there was something about Amos. She wanted him again.

CHAPTER TEN

Amos was absolutely NOT looking at Lucy as she sat at the King's knee. She was the last in the row of wives. The King was reading aloud from the Kingdom scripture, as he did every morning and Lucy's eyes were closed, her chin resting on her palm.

But Amos didn't even really notice that, because he wasn't looking at her. He hadn't looked at her as she'd walked down the hallway in that tight little excuse for a dress. He hadn't watched her whisper something in Zara's ear, making the girl smile. And he definitely hadn't watched as she'd gathered her long skirt around her to sit in her assigned chair.

Amos was losing his mortal mind. He could still taste her in his mouth. He felt so strange today, knowing that the best moment of his life was behind him now. He'd been to the mountaintop. It was face first between Lucy's legs. Amos discreetly adjusted himself in his pants.

He had to stop thinking about her. He had to put this behind him. Sure, it had been incredible. The hottest thing that would ever happen to him. But it was over. In the past. Actually, as far as he was concerned, it had never even happened.

Amos resolutely avoided her eyes, which were open again, and staring straight at him. He turned his head as he felt someone approach him from behind. Oh. Great. The fucking Oracle was here. Just what Amos needed.

The Oracle came to stand beside Amos and was obviously about to say hello, when a strange look came over his face. He leaned in and studied Amos's eyes. Amos immediately looked away, disconcerted by the weird stare and suddenly nervous that the Oracle could see more than he should.

The Oracle looked at Amos, then at Lucy. Then back to Amos. Amos turned away from him, supremely uncomfortable.

"Busy night?" The Oracle asked.

Amos turned and saw an expression on his face that could only be described as glee. Fuck. The Oracle knew something was up. How much he knew, Amos had no idea.

"Not really," he replied.

"Sure, sure," the Oracle said, scratching one hand over his stubble and staring at the side of Amos's face. "So that's her, huh?"

Amos grunted. Obviously the Oracle already knew the answer to that question. He was the one who'd picked her out of the 3 billion women on earth.

Amos could tell the Oracle was about to say more but he was blessedly interrupted when the King slapped his book closed. The reading of the scripture was over. Which meant that the King was going to address the room.

Usually the room was filled with many more people. But Lucy's presence required it just be Amos, the Oracle, the wives and a few other bodyguards in Amos's employ.

The King cleared his throat. "Lucy. Come here."

Amos held his breath at the defiant look on her face, but luckily she did as she was told.

"Kneel before me," the King said.

Again she did as she was told. Amos felt a weird twisting feeling in his stomach, watching her kneel before another man. He imagined himself in the King's position, Lucy eye level with his cock. Amos blew out a low breath and beside him the Oracle snickered.

Amos was so distracted he almost didn't notice the King pulling something out of a velvet covered box. The glinting of gold caught his eye.

His stomach dropped out when he realized what it was. It was her fidelity cuff. The King was going to put the choker around Lucy's neck the way he had for all of his wives. It would symbolize to all who she belonged to. Who owned her. Who got to sleep with her and impregnate her.

Amos felt sick. The King leaned down and dragged Lucy closer to him. She had been leaning away as far as she could get. Amos took a step forward.

Lucy was on all fours, having been pushed to the ground by the King. She was trying to crawl backwards, out of his grip. Amos took two more quick steps forward. But he felt something clamp onto his arm.

Turning, he saw the Oracle holding him back. But that's not what stopped him. He could have easily swatted the man aside. What stopped Amos in his tracks was the look on the Oracle's face. It was serious. More serious than Amos had ever seen him. The Oracle actually looked fearful at Amos's actions.

Amos shook free of him and turned back. He felt a roaring in his ears. The King had successfully clamped the golden cuff around Lucy's neck. Still on her knees, she dazedly had one hand on the choker, as if she couldn't believe it were real. Zara rushed forward and helped Lucy stand to go back to her chair.

King Dalyer reclined on the throne, he was slightly winded from the altercation, but Amos could see a flush of lust rise up the King's neck. Pushing Lucy to the ground and forcing the cuff around her neck had turned King Dalyer on.

For the second time Amos found himself walking forward and for the second time he felt the Oracle's fingers digging into his shoulder. The Oracle nodded his head to an alcove on the side of the hall. Amos looked back, saw that the King was once again reading from the scriptures, signaling the near close to the morning meeting.

Amos followed the Oracle, who immediately rounded on him once they were far enough to not be heard.

"Amos, have you lost your mind?" he whisper-shouted.

Pretty much. Yeah, he had. But Amos only grunted.

The Oracle scrubbed his face with his hands. "Amos, I don't know exactly what happened between you and Lucy, but I can tell you, if you keep going like this, it's gonna get you killed."

Amos knew that the Oracle could read the future. "Is that a fact?"

"No, it's a figure of fucking speech. Yes, it's fact!"

Amos had never seen the Oracle so agitated. "I don't know what you're talking about."

"Yes, Amos. You do. You know that there is an electric current running between you and Lucy. You know that you touched her last night. You know that you want to do it again. And that you can either completely ignore it and leave her to her fate with the King. Or..."

"Or what?"

"You tell me, Amos. What happens if you don't ignore it?"

Amos said nothing. If he didn't ignore it, then the King would have him executed. Simple as that. Amos's next thought was of the King pushing Lucy to the ground just then. That's what leaving her to her fate with the King was gonna look like. How could he ignore that?

"Amos," the Oracle started again, but Amos put up his hand.

"You don't know what the fuck you're talking about. There is nothing going on. Don't mention this to me ever again."

Amos stormed back into the hall, leaving the Oracle behind. He knew the Oracle was right and it pissed him off. He looked across the hall to where the wives, Lucy included, were rising as King Dalyer led them all to the meal hall. Breakfast time. Lucy looked pale and serious. It tugged at him.

The rest of the day passed that way. Perhaps it was because it was Lucy's first day, but the King kept his wives by his side the entire day. Never letting them speak with one another. Twice that day King Dalyer forced Lucy to kneel at his feet. He tugged his hands through her hair. Amos could see her wince at his rough hands.

Amos felt ripped in two different directions. On one hand, he had the King's best interests in mind. In that case he needed to ignore Lucy. On the other hand, he had Lucy's best interests at heart. In that case he needed to get Lucy the fuck out of there.

Finally, after the longest day of Amos's life, and he was sure Lucy's too, dinner was over. The King was tired. He dismissed his wives back to their chambers. Each wife was followed out of the hall by her specific bodyguard and Amos followed closely behind Lucy. He could feel the Oracle's eyes on his back. And more importantly he could feel King Dalyer's eyes on Lucy's back.

She hurried from the hall. But her movements were stiff and robotic. The second they got out of the big wrought iron doors, Lucy started to run in the direction of her room.

"Lucy!" Zara called.

But she didn't turn back. Amos raced after her, letting her stay ahead. He didn't want to interfere with her. He just needed to make sure she was safe. At first he wasn't sure if she was going to attempt to escape again. But she skidded to a stop outside of her quarters.

She ripped aside the curtain and started jamming her fingers onto all the different gems embedded in the wall. Fearing she was going to injure herself, Amos calmly pulled her away. He pressed the correct gem and the door swung open.

Lucy raced past him into the room. Her face was panicked and pale. She fell to her knees and clutched at her dress. Amos stepped out into the hallway. About to leave her to do whatever it was she was gonna do in there. He would lock her in and go back to his own chamber. She'd be safe that way. But then she turned to him, her chest heaving in desperation, her panting breaths coming quicker and quicker. Her eyes filling up half her face.

"Help me," she whispered.

He stepped into the room and slammed her door behind him. Falling to his knees next to her he gripped her by the shoulders, trying to figure out what was wrong.

"I can't breathe with this on," she gasped and clawed at the dress again. "It's too tight. Take it off, take it off."

She battled with the buttons down her back but her hands were shaking and nothing would tug free. He batted her hands away and she started to wheeze. She really couldn't breathe. He took two handfuls of the fabric on her back and ripped it apart. The dress tore cleanly down the seam. It fell to the ground, and revealed her gorgeously naked body.

Jesus Christ, what was he doing. Somehow he'd gotten her naked twice in 24 hours. He stood and tried to put some space between them, but she wasn't calming down. She rose halfway, but this time she was clutching the fidelity collar. She choked and gasped against it, trying to get her fingers underneath the tight gold.

"Choking me. Choking me," she coughed out.

He didn't think twice. He undid the heavy clasp in the back and ripped it off her neck. She took it from his hand and flung it across the room. He watched it arc away in slow motion. And to him, it was almost like it was his future flying away from him. Her fidelity to the King landed in a heavy thump on the carpet.

And there she was, gulping in air. Naked as the day she was born. Her panic was receding but her eyes filled with tears.

"I'll never wear that thing again," she whispered.

"Yes, hatchling, you will. You'll have to wear it every time you see him."

The tears overflowed her eyes. "How did this happen to me?"

He'd never remember exactly how, but somehow he was kneeling on the ground next to her. Hugging her tightly, one hand drawing circles on her back. The evening light of the setting sun slanted in through the thin windows that lined the very top of her room. The orange sunset across her light blue eyes made his heart constrict. Tears clung to her eyelashes and she was liquid and warm in his arms. He could feel the burn of her smooth skin through his clothes.

He had to leave now. Fuck, he had to go back in time and leave yesterday. That's how badly he had to leave. He needed to run back to the King and say something, anything, to get him to switch bodyguards back. He needed to go down to the village and find somebody to fuck. Get this out of his system. But first, he needed to get the hell out of this room.

He jerkily unhanded her and stood up. He took one step, two steps, backwards. She rose and stumbled away from him. She whipped on a red silk robe that hung in the wardrobe. He was both grateful and dismayed that she was covering herself up.

"I had a good life in Brooklyn," she said suddenly. "I had a good job, friends. I even had a boyfriend."

Amos scoffed at the memory of Dale. The blond dipshit who hadn't treated her well. But Lucy barreled on.

"I went to shows, watched TV whenever I wanted, and drank beer. I read books and met people in bars. I went to museums and took in art exhibitions that deeply moved me. I could have lived and died happily there." Tears rolled freely down her face and Amos couldn't look away from her.

She was talking about her humanity. Something that he'd helped the King steal from her. Something they'd completely disregarded in King Dalyer's desperate search for power. For the first time he saw King Dalyer through someone else's eyes. He saw an old man who would do morally questionable things to keep a title he might not deserve. He saw someone who pushed a woman to the ground. He saw someone who viewed Lucy as his possession. And not as the vivid, complicated person who was standing in front of him.

He knew then that he'd made his choice. The Oracle had already seen it. Why would Amos even pretend to fight it anymore. His DNA wouldn't allow him to ever cause harm to the King, but his heart was pledging its allegiance to Lucy.

He took a step toward her. Wanting to calm her. Wanting to hold her beautiful body in his arms. She stood in a shaft of the setting sun, dust motes floated around her, illuminating the air that had the honor of mingling with her scent.

"You did this to me," she said to him and he froze, halfway across the room. "You kidnapped me from my home, you monster. You planned it," she continued.

He didn't deny it. He couldn't look away from her. Anger colored her cheeks, brightened her eyes. Her hair hung in a messy wave down her back. The silk of the robe lovingly cradled her curves. His feet wouldn't move. He was immobilized by the truth of her words.

"You knew what the King was going to do to me. How he was going to treat me," she pointed at the collar on the floor. "And you dragged me here anyway."

"And now, I have to just wait here. Wait here for that disgusting piece of shit to come and get me pregnant." She crossed her arms under her chest and glared at him. Daring him to deny it.

"I won't let him." The words were out of Amos's mouth before he could swallow them back. What the fuck had he just said?

"What?" Lucy took a step back from him. "What did you just say?"

"I'm saying that I won't let the King touch you, hatchling." This time, Amos was saying the words with his whole self. He really meant them. His future was sealed the second he watched the King cuff her throat.

Amos started pacing back and forth. Combing his hand through his hair. "The portal doesn't open up again until the harvest moon in two months. Which, by the way," Amos looked up at her. "Is the same time he's gonna try to mate with you. He can't mate until the harvest moon."

Lucy shook her head at that bizarre piece of information. "I'll ask about that in a minute, but did you just say-,"

He cut her off, pacing and making plans. "So you're gonna have to endure it for two months. We can't let him know that we're trying to get you out. In the meantime the Oracle can keep searching for a replacement for you or maybe some sort of, I don't know..."

He trailed off when he realized Lucy was standing directly in front of him. She put her hands up to his chest to stop his pacing.

"Did you just say you were gonna protect me from him?"

Amos took a deep breath, nodded.

"You're not gonna let him touch me?"

His breath came out in a grunt. "Fuck, no."

Her entire demeanor changed. He realized it was a testament to how safe he made her feel. As soon as he promised to protect her, the tension left her body. Her lips parted and her eyes darkened. She dropped her gaze to his mouth. The front of her robe fell open just a little bit and Amos couldn't tear his eyes away from the slope of her soft breasts, pressing against one another.

"Are you gonna touch me?" she asked, her voice barely a whisper.

He let out a humorless chuckle. "I'm gonna get executed either way," he said. "So you better believe I'm gonna fuck you first."

CHAPTER ELEVEN

Amos considered jumping on her. Maybe lifting her up and sticking his tongue down her throat. But instead he stalked a slow circle around her. He sat down on the edge of the bed. Cocking his head to one side, he reached out and grabbed the knot at the front of her robe.

He dragged her closer and he felt the silk of the robe slide across her skin. His eyes dropped to her chest and his gaze darkened when he realized her nipples were standing up, pressing against the fabric.

Amos slid one finger along the seam of her robe, drawing goosebumps up on her skin. He twirled a finger through a loose lock of hair. Dragged that same finger up her neck.

"He touched you," Amos said, almost thoughtfully. He thought of every horrible moment that day.

She nodded. Her mouth pulling tight at the memory.

Amos stood up and walked into the bathroom. He quickly turned the taps on, adjusting for temperature. The enormous clawfoot tub started to fill. He came back out to the bedroom and held a hand out to her.

She walked to him and took his hand. The softness of her skin shot straight to his cock.

"First," he said and pushed the robe off of her shoulder. "I'm gonna wash you." He leaned down and swirled his tongue over her shoulder. "And then I'm gonna fuck you."

Her eyes dilated and he watched her clench her thighs together. She liked it when he said whatever the fuck he wanted to say.

He tugged at her and she followed him into the bathroom where curls of steam were coming from the bathwater. Pulling the chair in the corner over to the middle of the room, he sat down and faced her, lacing his hands behind his head.

"You're gonna strip that robe off for me. Nice and pretty."

Lucy nodded, her eyes huge and heavy with lust. She undid the knot in the front and dropped the belt onto the ground. Her eyes were begging for sex, her mouth full and pouty. The robe slipped off one shoulder, and with a shrug, the other. Lucy turned her back to Amos and let the robe slip even further. Her lower back was revealed. The robe slipped further.

Lucy let the robe drop completely.

"Come over here," Amos's voice ground out. Holy God. This woman was made to tempt him. He'd always appreciated women. Their curves and gracefulness always made him think about touching, tasting. But this woman was like a siren for him. One look at her and his entire body was like *why the fuck aren't we all they way inside that gorgeous creature.*

She crossed the room to him and he swooped her up in his arms in one motion. He turned off the taps and then gently set her in the water. Amos turned away from her and picked up a washcloth and soap. He started sudsing them together.

Lucy caught her lip in between her teeth. Maybe it was the motion of the water, or how desperately she needed to come, but her hand floated between her legs. Her thumb gently teased her clit and the sight drew Amos's eyes like a magnet. Then there was no more teasing. Her first two fingers plunged inside of her.

His eyes took in the expression on her face. Then they fell to her fingers buried inside her own wet heat.

"Fuck it," he said and tossed the cloth over his shoulder. He ripped his shirt off over his head.

Now that his days were basically numbered, he needed to get this show on the road. No more tempting, no more teasing. No more bullshit. He ripped his pants and shoes off and then he was standing naked before her for the first time.

She gasped at the sight of him, one hand covering her mouth. He looked down to see what she was gasping at, but all he saw was his regular body. His muscles created dark shadows of definition. A light smattering of body hair covered him over.

He supposed she was probably gasping at the sight of his manhood, standing at full attention for her. Lucy sat in the tub, working her fingers into herself. But she paused and looked up at him.

"Amos, I don't think it's gonna fit."

He laughed and didn't give her long to worry about it. He was suddenly on top of her in the tub, water overflowing the sides. Instantly his cock was sliding through her wet folds. Her hands fisted on his back as she tried to take him inside, but he wouldn't let her. He speared his hand through her hair and dragged her mouth to his. Her pussy slipped and slid along the side of the taut skin of his cock as she opened her mouth to his.

His tongue pressed insistently into her mouth. Their first kiss, he realized. Her taste exploded in him and he had the weirdest feeling of coming home. He knew they'd never kissed before, but somehow, it was like her taste was made for him.

One of his hands dragged down her side and cupped her breast. His thumb strummed over her nipple and her back arched.

"You have no idea how badly I've needed to touch you," he said into her mouth.

They rolled in the tub and they were on their sides, slipping and sliding against one another.

"Your body was made to be touched," he said and water from the tub splashed over their faces and hair. He dropped his head to her nipple, slightly under water and clamped his mouth over it. He suckled her. Hard.

Lucy screamed out and the sound made him even harder. He came up for air and flipped her over so that her stomach lay on the bottom of the bath. He lay himself down on top of her and let his cock slide against her pussy from the back. He let one of his hands go under her to trail to her clit. He drew circles around it.

Nipping one of her earlobes in his teeth he whispered in her ear. "Your body was made to be sucked on."

She moaned and pushed her ass back into him. He felt the head of his cock spear through her wetness but not inside. He pulled himself away.

"We're all washed off now," he said tersely and stood, water streaming off of him. He reached down and pulled her to standing. They stepped out of the tub together.

Grabbing a towel from the hook, Amos boosted her so that she sat on the bathroom counter. He dragged the towel over her body and then his own. But he couldn't take it anymore. He gripped the back of her neck and pulled her in for a kiss.

Their tongues warred with each other. She bit at his lips and their teeth clicked. He tipped her head back further because he wasn't in far enough yet. He pushed himself between her legs and they were perfectly lined up. The head of his cock pressed into her a half an inch.

"Condom?" she blearily asked.

"There'll be some by your bed," he said and lifted her up so that her legs came around his waist.

"Just so you know," she said as he sucked on her neck. "I'm clean."

"Dragons don't get stds," he said as he walked her across the bathroom. "And just so you know, I can't get you pregnant until the harvest moon." At some point he was gonna have to explain that one to her. "But better safe than sorry," he said.

But she ground herself against him, pressing her wetness to his stomach and he couldn't go any farther. He paused and pressed her against the wall.

They slid against one another again and this time she tilted her hips and caught him just inside.

"Fuck," he said and pressed himself in a little further.

Lucy's head fell back and she bit back a scream.

"Oh god," she moaned.

Nothing had ever felt this good before. She pushed down on him a little further.

"Condom," he bit out. And stepped away from the wall, but he stayed pressed into her. He took a step out toward the bedroom and she pressed down on him a little further.

He stopped walking and flexed his hips, grabbing her around the waist and pushing her down on his cock. They both groaned at the inch he pushed in. This was the most torturous ecstasy he'd ever felt. From the look on her face it was mutual.

He took a few more quick steps toward the bed and each one pushed him further and further in. He reached the edge of the bed and set her down.

They stayed where they were, gripping one another so tightly, their tongues insistently pressing together. He reached out and fumbled with a side drawer next to her bed. Digging through it he came out with a condom.

She wiggled her hips and opened her legs even wider.

"Fuck, Lucy. You're killing me." He held the condom in front of them and tried to tear it, but she reached out for it at the same time. It got knocked out of their hands and to the floor.

Amos looked at the condom, five feet away. He looked at Lucy. Her eyes hooded with lust, her lips parted and swollen. Panting for him. He looked at where their two bodies were partially joined. He was covered in her juices, half in, half out. She put her hands on her knees and pulled them to the sides, opening herself fully to him.

"Fuck it," he said again. And plunged into her. Lucy's back arched off the bed and she screamed her pleasure. The walls echoed with it.

"God, you're so big. Baby, you're so big," she moaned, her head whipping from side to side.

He gave her a second to get used to his size, but then he pulled out almost all the way. He slammed back into her, figuring they'd been teasing each other enough over the last day. Finding his rhythm, he really started to move. He put one knee on the edge of the bed, but his other foot stayed on the ground. He pushed against it to keep himself stable.

The bed, heavy as it was, started to inch across the carpet with each thrust he gave her.

"So tight," he groaned against her shoulder. He pressed his eyes closed so hard that colors flashed among the black of his eyelids. Sweat broke out over his back. She started moving her hips to meet his thrusts and their combined movements intensified the sensations.

"Yes," she moaned. "I'm gonna- oh god- I'm gonna..."

But her words abruptly cut off as her back arched completely off the bed and her arms and legs gripped him almost as tight as her pussy was. Her breasts crushed into his chest. Her orgasm had her clamping down on him like a tight fist. Her eyes dilated with intense pleasure and her lips opened into a perfect O.

He had to kiss that. Clamping his mouth over hers he rolled them to their sides and continued pumping into her. He slid a hand between them and tugged at one of her nipples. She screamed again and ground herself into him even harder. She was clamping down on him again and he was pretty sure she was either still coming or coming again.

He flipped them, this time so that she was on top and he watched the hottest scene he'd ever seen in his life.

Her head fell back as her hands curled into fists on his chest. She pulled up off of him for a second and then plunged back down. And then she did it again. He could feel every tight, wet inch of her. Feel himself bottoming out inside of her. This was it. It was almost unbearable pleasure as he built toward his release. Her breasts bounced and he had to touch them.

His hands on her seemed to bring her back to earth a little and her eyes focused in on him again. She started to ride him even faster. He was racing toward the edge. Wanting more for her, he dropped one hand to her clit and started gently rolling it under one thumb. And then she was gone again. Her eyes, unseeing and dilated, rolled upwards.

Her pussy clamped down on his cock even harder than before. She fell forward on his chest and he rolled them over one last time. He pushed into from the top and rode her for all he was worth. The room filled with the slap of skin on skin. Their chests smashed firmly against one another. They slipped and slid through the wetness they'd created together.

She was moaning nonsense words in his ear as she arched into him again. "Amos," she whispered his name.

And he came, pumping furiously into her. His entire world shrunk down to one spot in between their legs. The place where they were joined together. As if they were one being. For a few gloriously pleasurable moments, as he came and came, there was no line between them. It was blurred and disappeared by their passion for one another. Their pleasure combined them together. They were one animal, together, crying out from the sharpest ecstasy either of them had ever felt.

CHAPTER TWELVE

Lucy lay in a stupor for who knows how long afterward. She faced Amos, whose face was shaded by blue shadows. His hand traced patterns on her back.

"I have to go shift for a little while, hatchling" he said quietly.

"It's a need?" she asked, curious.

"Sometimes. It can always be controlled. But the urge gets stronger now and then."

"It's very strong right now?"

He nodded. "Things get... simpler in dragon form. Everything is more black and white. A dragon's passions run really high. Nothing is ever wishy-washy. It makes it easy to figure out how to feel about something that's confusing in human form."

"And you're confused right now?"

"Lucy, I don't think you understand." He pulled her onto his chest and stroked her hair back. "Protecting the King, loyalty to the King, isn't just my job. It's my birthright. My ancestors have done this for centuries. The urge to be loyal to the royal line has been bred into me. It's in my DNA. It was a compulsion for me when I was a child, even." He paused and Lucy wondered if he was going to go on. "And I just completely turned my back on that. No," he scrubbed his hands over his face. "Actually I swan dove away from it."

Lucy was quiet for a long while. She really hadn't realized quite how far Amos's duty stretched. She might not have pushed him so hard if he had. She just thought he was like dragon secret service. She didn't think he was compelled by his heritage.

She thought back on their last 45 minutes and blushed deeply. She wasn't really a blusher. Amos noticed immediately and ran a finger over her cheek.

"Reminiscing?" he asked and grinned.

Lucy was momentarily blinded by his smile. She'd never seen it before. It changed his entire face. Crinkled his eyes and flashed his white teeth. Made him achingly handsome.

She leaned forward and kissed him. But she didn't let it draw out. Pulling back, she was immensely pleased by the lust in his eyes. She could really draw it out of him.

"Can I come?" She asked.

He raised an eyebrow suggestively. "I thought you already did,"

She rolled her eyes. "No, I mean I want to come see you shift. I want to see your full dragon."

He searched her eyes. "Are you sure? It might be scary."

She stared him in the eye. "I'm not exactly a shrinking violet, Amos."

He chuckled. "I'm not familiar with that human colloquialism, but I'm sure you're not a shrinking violet." He reached out and played with a lock of her hair, still damp from their bath. "You're a toughie."

She flopped backwards. "I used to think I was, but these last few days have really put me through the ringer."

Amos got up and rifled through her wardrobe. "Wear this, it'll be cold on the roof."

He tossed a fur lined coat onto the bed and walked to the bathroom to pull his own clothes on.

Lucy got up and looked through the wardrobe for the first time by herself. Fancy dress, fancy dress, fancy dress. She sighed inwardly. Nothing that she would wear. But spying a small drawer on the side she pulled it open and dug through it.

"Perfect!" she exclaimed happily as she discovered the soft pants and shirt. They were made of a soft fleecy material and she was fairly certain they were underclothes, but better than the Victorian era dresses that she couldn't even breathe in.

She pulled her clothes on and turned around to find Amos standing in the middle of the room, holding the fidelity cuff in his hands.

She automatically took a step back from it. Amos's eyes looked sad and weary.

"You have to wear it whenever you leave the room, hatchling. Otherwise the King will take it as a sign of your infidelity to him. A rejection."

She took another step away. "I do reject him. I'm not faithful to him. I just slept with you for fuck sake!"

Her voice rose. Amos tossed the collar onto a side table and came over to her. He held her face still and looked deep into her eyes. Lucy took a deep breath and let him calm her down.

"Lucy. I know that. You know that. But the King cannot know that. If he suspects us before we can get you out of here, he'll execute me instantly. And I can't protect you if I'm dead."

Lucy felt all the air leave her chest. She gripped Amos's shirt in her hands so tight her knuckles went white.

"You were serious about that? Protecting me could get you executed?"

He nodded. "It could. We'd be directly defying a tyrant's orders. We'd be ruining his chances at continuing his family line. I'd be betraying him..." Amos trailed off under the weight of his words.

"How can we do it so you don't get killed?" she asked.

He smiled a little. "There's someone we can talk to about that. Who can help us. I think. But in the meantime, you can wear the cuff and act like nothing has changed."

She could still feel the strangling weight of the disgusting object around her neck. But what Amos said made sense. She had to keep the illusion up.

Suddenly Amos's eyes lit up. "I have an idea."

He strode across the room and picked up the collar. He brought it back over to her.

"How would you feel about wearing it if it didn't symbolize fidelity to the King?" he asked.

"What do you mean?"

He snicked out one of his dragon claws on his fingers and Lucy watched in fascination. She couldn't wait to see him shift fully. He dragged his claw across the gold on the inside of the collar. A screeching sound made her wince, but she couldn't take her eyes away.

"This is a dragon's eye," he said handing her the collar to inspect the etching he'd just scratched on. It was an oval with an x through the middle. "It's something dragon children do." He smiled a little. "It's an oath. Signing it is like signing your name to a contract. Only instead of a contract, it's a promise."

"A promise," she mused and flipped the collar over. On the outside it was still King Dalyer's fidelity cuff of heavy decorated gold. She turned it back. But on the inside it was smooth and plain, adorned only with the childlike etching. Amos's promise to keep the King away from her.

She put it around her neck. And he helped her clasp it. The metal was smooth and cool, except for the slightly rough etching. She felt none of the trapped feeling of panic from when she wore it before. She concentrated on the secret promise, pressing gently against her. With her always.

Amos looked pleased as he watched her play with the cuff. He picked up the fur coat and helped her into it.

"You're wearing undergarments, you know."

"I figured," she said. "But there was nothing else in there that I wanted to wear!"

"Maybe the other wives have other clothes you could borrow."

They both inwardly cringed at the word, "other". It just reminded them that Lucy was part of that count.

A slightly chagrined look came over Amos's face as he led her to the door. "You're gonna have to go out first and make sure there's no one passing by."

"Why?" she asked, cocking her head to one side.

"Because I'm not supposed to be in your chambers. And I don't want to be seen coming out in the dead of the night."

"Because then everyone will know that you just fucked me silly and made me come for like eight straight minutes?" she asked sweetly, batting her eyes at him.

He chuffed out a surprised laugh and pulled her in for a quick kiss. "Exactly."

"Fair enough," she shrugged and did as he asked, pulling open the door and peeking out in the hallway. "All clear."

The fortress was much larger than she had thought. He led her through a few different secret passageways and stairwells. She thought he might be taking her an intentionally circuitous route to avoid running into anyone that shouldn't be seeing them together.

She sagged against a wall as they came to the bottom of yet another set of stairs. "For the love of god, Amos. I can't."

He grinned at her, scooping her up in his arms. Her heart stuttered.

"This is how I carried you when you first came out of the portal."

"I was fighting you as hard as I could."

"It was cute."

"Cute!" She crossed her arms. "I was going for aggressive and intimidating."

"Maybe it would have been for a human man," he shrugged.

"I guess I'll have to try it out and get back to you."

"No," he growled, his eyes dark. "I don't want you to wiggle around in a human man's arms. Or anyone's arms but mine," he amended fiercely. But his eyes softened when he looked down and saw her trailing her finger along the gold collar.

She opened her mouth to respond to him, but all words cut short when he kicked open a final door and they stepped out onto a windy roof. The night sky opened above them like a humongous glass chandelier.

There were three times as many stars than Lucy had ever seen before. And the sky somehow looked deeper than on earth. As if it were more three dimensional than normal.

He set her gently down and she found she had been holding her breath. She turned a small circle, her head toward the sky and gasped in pleasure when a shooting star went burning through the air. The tail was the color of an aurora borealis, green leading to aqua to violet. She clapped her hands over her mouth in wonder. It was so beautiful she felt like she could open her mouth and taste it.

A whooshing sound came from directly behind her and she turned. She froze in her tracks when she found she was staring directly into the eyes of the largest creature she'd ever seen. He was a lot faster at transforming than the King. He'd done it in seconds, and silently.

She stood still and took him in. His eyes were the light yellow-green of spring leaves and catlike, each as large as a goose egg. But his predominant color was the clear, glassy amber of his scales. The same as the color of his human eyes. The scales on his humongous back and belly were as large as dinner plates, but they gave way to smaller ones on his arms and legs.

His head towered above her as tall as a giraffe and his tail, she realized was curled around where she stood. She turned a circle trying to see the whole thing. A humongous iridescent spike shot out of the end. It was made of a material Lucy couldn't even imagine. Obviously biological, but clear, like glass. She moved toward it, her hand outstretched, but he instantly jerked it away. The heavy tail thumping on the ground as he dragged it.

"Poison," he said and his voice made Lucy tremble. She'd never heard anything like it in her life. It was Amos's voice, but so many octaves lower she felt the bass of it in her chest. It was almost scary.

She turned back to face the impressive beast.

"You can actually fly?" she asked, her mind spinning in wonder at all the new things she was seeing.

He stretched his wings out behind him and Lucy gasped. They had to be at least twenty feet long and eight feet high at their tallest part. With a great stirring of the air, he beat his wings, once, twice and he was airborne. For such a large creature, he flew with incredible grace, first gaining altitude and then speed as he dipped and soared through the air. Lucy tracked his movements across the sky, her head whipping from one side the next.

It almost looked as if he were dipping in between the stars, but that must have been an illusion. She watched in utter joy and amazement. It looked like he really had needed to shift. He both danced and dipped as if he were immensely enjoying it. But he also performed the quick, methodical sprints of a dedicated runner. Someone who exercised for sanity.

She pulled the fur coat around her and laid down on the stone roof. The stars spun above her and her eyes grew heavy as the great creature disappeared into the deep black of the sky, only to reappear with a flash of the moonlight on his scales. For all the intensity of the last few hours, she'd never felt a peace like this.

CHAPTER THIRTEEN

Amos hadn't been lying to Lucy when he told her that things were clearer when he was in dragon form. Issues that had gray, blurry lines suddenly crystallized. They became defined as his predominant feelings took over and the smaller, complicating ones fell away.

Amos swooped in and out of the air pockets, letting the currents guide his path. The air was crystal cold and fresh so high up in the sky. He opened his enormous, vicious teeth and let a wisp of a cloud slide over his tongue. Flipping over in the air, he executed a fierce dive, plummeting back toward earth, and it seemed, toward his fate.

What had seemed so confusing to him in his human form became vividly clear to him. But it was hard to look at, almost like opening his eyes to the bright sun after spending years in a dark cave.

On the one side of his life was the King. And on the other was Lucy. In his human form, when he thought of them, he stood in the middle tugged back and forth over his loyalty to them. But in his dragon form, he stood in the middle only to protect Lucy.

The King was his past. Lucy was his future. As short of a future as that might be, he chose her. He'd choose her again and again. He knew what that meant. He knew what Lucy meant to him. If she were a dragon, he'd assume that he meant the same to her. But as she was human, he didn't know. How did humans fall in love? It seemed like sometimes they didn't even know if they were or not.

By the time Amos's wings grew tired and he was ready to shift back to his human form, he wasn't confused anymore. But he was sad. His whole identity was tied up in loyalty to the King. His father's identity as well.

As he plummeted back toward the roof of the fortress where Lucy waited for him, he began to transform in mid air. It was something he'd taught himself to do as a kid. He landed gently on his human feet, his wings folding up into nothing and he was full human again. He missed his father. Having the same mission, the same job as he had always connected Amos to the memory of his dad. He suddenly felt naked without it.

Not to mention the fact that he was actually naked on the rooftop. And it was cold. He hurried back over to where he'd lain his clothes. He expected Lucy to make some comment about it, but he realized that she'd fallen asleep, her coat covering her like a blanket.

She amazed him. He'd never met a stronger person in his entire life. How she was reconciling all of this in her mind he'd never know. All he knew was that now that he'd seen her spirit, there was no un-seeing it. There was no turning away from her.

Fully dressed now, Amos bent and picked her up. He carefully padded back through the castle, keeping an eye out for anyone who might see them. A shaft of moonlight splashed in from a window. Amos was so absorbed in the color it turned Lucy's hair that he didn't notice Zara peeking at them from behind a red tapestry. A small smile ghosted over her serious face and she sighed as she melted back into her room.

Lucy awoke as Amos lowered her onto the bed. She sat up to gently tug her arms free of the fur coat. Amos tossed it over a chair and pulled back the covers for her to crawl under. She held her arms out to him and he only hesitated for a second before kicking off his shoes and pants, shrugging out of his shirt, and crawling in beside her.

Her head instantly came to rest on his chest.

"Did things become clearer for you in your dragon form?" she asked.

"Yes." He nodded, not sure how to talk to her about what he'd come to understand. That he was pledging himself to her for as long as he lived. She waited expectantly but he wasn't quite ready to get into the details. "I've never fallen asleep next to a woman before."

"Really? You've never had a girlfriend before?"

"No. The men in my family don't have girlfriends or wives. We often have partners for occasional...fun. But we only mate for offspring to keep the line going."

Lucy was quiet for a minute. He could practically feel her absorbing that information. "So your mother..."

He shrugged. It was an old absence that wasn't nearly as ragged or hungry as when he'd been a boy. "A woman I've never met. My father only met her the night she became pregnant with me. My father raised me. That's common with dragons."

"They're raised by their fathers?"

"Yes and no. Dragon shifter children are often raised as apprentices by the parent with the more important, more prestigious, occupation. The other parent gives up rights to that child. It's... often complicated. But most people respect the cultural rules around it."

"That's really weird," Lucy said. She sat up and looked at him. "There's nothing wrong with single parent households. My mother raised me by herself. But to have two parents there and capable and for one of them to have absolutely no contact with the kid for no other reason than whose job is more important? I know we're different species and we have different expectations, but that is really weird."

He laughed a little, rubbing her back until she laid back down. "It's not quite as bad as you think. Dragons are compelled by duty. We need jobs and missions. Human children need to play with and be nurtured by their parents. Dragon children need to be trained, taught, and given jobs by their parents. It registers as affection. I swear," he added when he saw her skeptical expression.

She shrugged. "Okay. I guess I'll believe it when I see it."

His heart raced a little bit at that statement and he cleared his throat. He wondered what she meant. Did she mean it figuratively? Or did she mean when she had a dragon child herself? His? Suddenly the dragon custom of single parent raising seemed as weird to him as it did to her. If she were to have a child by him, he couldn't imagine cutting her out of the equation. It would be one of the greatest joys of his life to see her with their child.

He cleared his throat again. That was utterly ridiculous. First of all, there was no chance of them raising a child together. Either he was going to succeed in getting her back through the portal and then he was going to be executed. Or he was going to fail at getting her through the portal and he'd be executed. Either way, the result was the same.

Second of all, things had become clear for him in dragon form. But that didn't mean she felt the same way. His dragon heart was much more passionate than a typical human heart. From what he understood humans could date and be intimate with partners they weren't even really that in to.

Take the absolute dickhead she'd just dumped. By all indications she'd spent a great deal of time with him before deciding he wasn't her cup of tea.

Amos knew how he felt in his heart. But he didn't know how Lucy felt. He guessed it was time to clear that up. He opened his mouth but she interrupted him.

"What's the deal with this?" she asked, running her finger over the diamond stud in his earlobe.

"My earring?" he asked, confused.

"Yeah, it's pretty nineties."

"You mean it's not in style on earth?"

"Not unless you're a member of a boy band," she said, grinning.

He hadn't the slightest idea what a boy band was but he didn't like the sound of it. "I'm not a boy. Maybe I'm part of man band."

Lucy burst out laughing and fell backwards. "That's definitely not a thing. But seriously, why do you and all your security goons wear them? It can't be just a style choice."

He ran his finger over it again, suddenly feeling like he had to defend it a little bit. "Most dragon men wear them. It's not a style choice, it's a dragon thing."

She propped her head up on her hand. "Dragon thing?"

"Sure. Try and think about the things you've heard about dragons."

Her eyes went to one side as she tried to remember. "Let's see. What do I know about dragons. Oh! They really like treasure. Is that it?" she asked, beaming at her discovery.

He met her smile and nodded. "Yeah. Dragons all really have a thing for jewels. Everyone wears them or keeps them close at all times. It's not an actual source of power for us, but it's a kind of comfort. We feel naked without it."

She ran her finger over the stud. He smiled when she impulsively leaned forward and kissed it.

"Ok," she said. "Then I can live with it. What about other dragon legends. Are they true?"

"Like what?"

"Like, you know." She opened her mouth and breathed out hard, her fingers waving like a claw in front her mouth.

"What the hell is that?" he asked, totally confused.

"Breathing fire!" she exclaimed, exasperated that she didn't get her charade.

"Oh. Yeah. We can do that."

"What? Really?! That is so frickin cool. I wish I could do that."

"No you don't," he said, amused by her enthusiasm.

"Why?"

"We can only do it when our mates are threatened. And apparently it hurts like hell."

She looked up at him thoughtfully. "You use it to protect your mates? I thought dragons didn't care about their mates very much."

"What?" Nothing could be farther from the truth.

"Well, when you explained the whole single parent thing, I just assumed it meant that you didn't care about-," she waved her hand in the air to symbolize whatever it was she couldn't put into words.

"I see how you could have thought that, but trust me. It's not how I meant to say it. Most of the time a dragon chooses to become pregnant with someone who isn't important to them. They do it because that other person is the right choice to keep their family line strong and healthy. The way my father did with my biological mother."

"The way the King wants to do with me."

Amos nodded tersely and moved on, not wanting to talk about that. "But that's not what I mean when I say 'mate'. When dragons take a mate, a true mate, there is nothing more important to them than that other dragon. When dragons take a true mate, they are setting aside all other things. All their duties, all the things they were born to do. It's all consuming. And inconvenient. And rare. Most dragons choose not to even search for it. Because it disrupts the order so much."

"How does it disrupt the order?"

Amos searched for the words. "True mates typically raise their offspring together as a family. They don't choose one parent to apprentice the child. And they become deeply protective of their family unit. The true mates will fight and die for one another and their children. It creates tensions in the community. It's why most dragons don't go looking for their true mate. They only take up with them if they *happen* to meet and have no other choice but to bond and mate."

"No other choice? You say it like you come under a spell or something."

"It's almost like a spell." Amos traced a hand over her hair. Only a few days ago he would have been speaking hypothetically. But now, feeling her soft weight draped over him, smelling her light, powdery smell, he spoke from experience. "You try to fight it at first, to keep your life the way it was. But every molecule in your body pushes you toward that person."

He leaned forward and gently kissed her lips.

"You try to take a step away," he continued. "But you find yourself taking a step closer."

She let out a slow breath that washed over his face. "You're talking like you've been through it."

"Actually I kind of wanted to talk to you about that."

"About what?" She raised her head up off his chest and rested her chin on one fist.

"About what I realized when I was in my dragon form. What came clear for me." He twisted a lock of her hair around his fingers. Her eyes were light blue

pools of light and he felt like she could see right
through to his heart.

"Yes..." she prompted, obviously impatient to
hear what he was having so much trouble finding the
words for.

He reached behind her neck and unhooked the
fidelity cuff they'd both forgotten she was wearing.
He flipped it over in one hand and ran his finger over
the dragon's eye he'd drawn on. "I was wondering if
maybe the cuff could symbolize something more than
just my promise to keep you safe."

"What else?" She reached out to trace the eye as
well and their fingers whispered past one another.
Her guileless eyes took up her whole face.

"I want it to symbolize your fidelity to me."

His eyes searched hers for reaction and he was
surprised and a little incensed when he saw
disappointment there.

She sat up, the covers falling away from her. "Of
course I'm going to be faithful to you, Amos. Who the
hell else would I sleep with?"

He cocked his head to one side, confused by her
anger. "Ok. Why did that make you mad?"

"It didn't." She shook her head and pinched the
bridge of her nose. "It really didn't. I just thought,
after that whole conversation, that you were gonna
tell me something else right there. And I guess I was
disappointed when you said the fidelity thing."

"What did you think I was going to tell you?"

She covered her face with her hands. "It's too
embarrassing."

He reached forward and pried her hands away.
"Lucy. Tell me."

She looked down at the covers and played with them absentmindedly. "I guess I thought that you were gonna tell me that I was your true mate."

Either his chest constricted or his heart grew. He wasn't sure. But he had to kiss the sweetness off of her lips. He gently brought her face to his and rolled them over so that she was pinned underneath him.

"Lucy, you're missing the most important part of the title 'true mate'. It's 'mate'. You couldn't be my true mate unless you got pregnant by me."

She looked up at him. An emotion crossing her face that he couldn't read. Wanted desperately to be able to, but couldn't.

CHAPTER FOURTEEN

Lucy woke up alone the next morning. And for every morning for the next month. She knew she would. Each night, Amos would sneak into her room. He'd make intense, holy love to her and sneak out before the morning.

Lucy had never been so happy and so sad in her entire life. Her days were filled with drab monotonous pretending. Pretending she wasn't completely disgusted by King Dalyer. Pretending she was faithful to him. Pretending she was getting used to being counted among his wives. She dreaded it with her whole soul. Her days were marked only by her prayers for them to go faster.

But her nights were marked by intense, ecstatic pleasure. And safety. And wild love.

The love part she'd only begun to admit to herself. She felt that it was utterly useless to deny. She could feel it coursing off of her in waves toward him, even when he stood forty feet away in the King's chambers. Even though they were good at hiding it, it was a miracle to her that other people couldn't sense the intensity between them.

She wondered if the other wives might suspect something. Especially Zara, whom Lucy had come to know as incredibly smart and observant. The other two wives, Beatrix and Sara, were much less interested in Lucy. In fact, they'd barely acknowledged her for the first two weeks they were forced to coexist.

Lucy assumed it was because of the bias that so many dragon shifters had against humans, but Zara had corrected her on that.

"No," Zara had said. "It's not because you're a human, it's because they don't want to get attached to you. There have been other wives. Ones King Dalyer has been less patient with than me and Beatrix and Sara. It's always really hard when he decides he's done with them."

"Done with them?" Lucy had asked, feeling sick.

"Yes. King Dalyer is merciful though. He always executes very quickly."

In a way, Lucy hated any extra information she ever got about King Dalyer. It made her days with him so much harder. It was almost impossible not to flinch away from him. But she knew it was even harder for Amos to watch the King paw at her. She could feel Amos's fiery, furious energy anytime the King even spoke to her.

And their sex had become more and more intense in response. Any day that the King had touched her, Amos would wash her that night. He was always so thorough. His hands touching every part of her body, he'd wash away any memory of the King. But once he was inside her, the gentleness would disappear.

"Mine," he'd chant in her ear, tugging on her nipples and riding her into orgasm. She would lose count of the number of times he'd make her come every night. She came on his hands, on his face, on his cock. They had sex on every surface of her room. Sometimes falling asleep on the floor, in the bathtub, sitting up against the door.

But every morning she'd wake up tucked into her bed. And she'd know he stood outside of her door, pretending he'd just arrived for his morning shift.

This particular morning, Lucy wasn't dreading the day quite as much as she usually did. It was Sunday. The one day of the week that the King didn't require the wives to sit dutifully at his knee. They were allowed to take care of their affairs and do as they wished around the fortress.

Lucy and Zara had taken to spending those Sundays together. Usually going up to the roof where Amos had taken her before. Zara's dragon form was so beautiful and Lucy loved to watch her shift. To watch her dip and fly among the clouds.

"What you need is a saddle," Lucy said to Zara as she sat in the sun next to her.

"A saddle? Like, those things humans use on horses?" Zara asked, confused.

"Yeah, you need a dragon saddle. And then I could ride on your back."

Zara flopped down and laughed. "Uh, no thanks, human. I'll pass on being your horse."

"Not so you could take me around to any old place. I mean so that I could learn what it feels like to fly."

Zara smiled. "Flying is really great, but Lucy, it's not worth the risk. Saddle or not, my scales would absolutely flay you alive if you slipped against them."

"I know, I know," Lucy pouted. "They're sharp." She'd had the exact same conversation with Amos and he'd reacted the same way. First in outrage at the indignity of a human riding him, and then in horror at imagining what his dragon form would do to her fragile human body.

"Maybe you could ask Amos," Zara said, somewhat nervously. "I'll bet he'd let you."

"Why do you say that?" Lucy asked stiffly.

"Because he would do anything for you."

Lucy stayed quiet, totally unsure of what to say. She was pretty sure that Zara would never rat her out. But Amos's life hung in the balance. Pretty sure was not good enough.

"I would never tell anyone, Lucy." Zara whispered, her eyes serious.

"I don't know what you're talking about, Zara." Lucy kept her eyes on the sky above her.

"He's a good man, Lucy. I've known him my whole life. He's gonna get you out of here. I just know it. I just wish I could come with you." Zara's voice was almost a whisper at the end.

Lucy's heart broke cleanly in two and she gripped Zara's hand.

"Couldn't you?" Lucy knew she was blowing her cover, but the weight of Zara's situation fell on her all at once. This poor girl was just waiting, ticking away the days until she became old enough for the King to consummate.

Zara's eyes were sad as she shook her head. "I can't go through the portal until I'm 20. The portal only allows dragon shifters in their human forms to go through in either direction. So I wouldn't make it."

Lucy cocked her head to one side. "But you're in your human form right now."

Zara blushed and shook her head. "Not everywhere."

"Um. What?" Lucy was more confused than ever.

Zara blushed even further. "Dragon girls keep scales... down there. Until they are about 20, when they disappear on their own. It's to keep men away from us. To keep us from procreating while we're too young to be mothers. But it also means we're in a constant state of half shift. And can't go through the portal."

Lucy tried to school her face into a reasonable expression, to not make Zara feel bad. But whoa. "Scales on your hoo-ha, huh? Welp, that'll definitely keep your virginity intact."

Zara burst into giggles and Lucy followed, relieved she hadn't offended her.

"I'll miss you, Lucy," Zara said, her eyes sad again.

Lucy just gripped her hand, her brain churning a mile a minute. They stayed like that for a long time until the afternoon light lengthened across the roof. Neither of them wanted their King-less Sunday to end, but they knew it was time to head back to their separate chambers. Lucy felt even more reluctant than usual to let Zara out of her sight. She was just so young and sweet.

Zara needed somebody to look after her. And that night as she brushed her hair, Lucy decided that she was the perfect person to do that. She took a deep breath and knew what she needed to do. Amos was not going to like this. Lucy heard the door to her chamber slide open and knew Amos was there. She paused in brushing her hair and held up a hand to stop him as he slid down to give her a kiss.

"I want to stay in the realm for four more years," she said.

Amos stepped back as if she'd slapped him. "What are you talking about?"

"I don't want to leave until we can take Zara with us."

Understanding lit his eyes. "And she can't go through the portal until she's twenty."

Lucy nodded. "So if we make just a few minor tweaks to our plan-," she started.

"Minor tweaks! Hatchling, four additional years are not minor tweaks to the plan."

"Well, why don't we go hide someplace in the Kingdom for four years?" She threw her arms out wide. "It's a big place, we can find someplace where the King won't be able to find us."

Amos pinched the bridge of his nose. "Hatchling, do you understand the resources the King has at his disposal? He has an Oracle for god sakes. And a 15,000 man army that's ready to march tomorrow. He's the most powerful being in the dragon realm. There is no hiding from him."

"Ok, fine. If we can't hide from him in the dragon realm somewhere, then we stay here. In the castle, and just tough it out for four years." She turned back to face the mirror and brush her hair, unwilling to look at his face as she said those words.

He was stone silent and she could feel the tension rolling of him.

"Tough what out, hatchling?"

Lucy said nothing. He could fill in the blanks by himself.

He came up behind her and took the brush out of her hand. Studied her in the mirror of the vanity. His gaze was fiery and she couldn't look away from the fury she saw there.

"I said, 'tough what out'? Tough out us hiding our relationship? Tough out him pushing you to the ground and making you do his bidding? Tough out him fucking you whenever he feels like it for the next four years? Tough out him impregnating you? Tough out the fact that I fucking hate him now? That I was born to protect him but I want to rip his fucking throat out whenever he looks at you? Is that what you want to tough out for the next four years?"

"Amos," she started, but she didn't get to finish talking. He reached down and ripped her dress off over her head. He stared at her in the mirror. He was clothed and hulking behind her completely naked body. He roughly cupped one of her breasts. Her eyes dropped to the sight in the mirror.

"You think we can keep hiding this?" His other hand dropped to her pussy, cupping her. She knew he could feel how wet she was when his eyes dilated in the mirror.

"How long do you think we can keep pretending that you don't come on my cock every night of the week?" Every muscle in Lucy's abdomen clamped down at those words and she felt a rush of heat start to slide down her thighs. She looked up at his chiseled face. He was looking at her with so much intensity in his brown eyes. His lips were set with desire for her. She reached back to touch him and was delighted when he leaned into it like an overgrown cat.

But he wasn't waylaid by her touch for long. He tugged on one nipple and then the next, making them stand up at full attention. She could feel his cock pressing into her back.

"This thing between us just keeps getting stronger. How long do you think we can hide it? The Oracle knows, the wives are starting to suspect. It won't be long before the King knows. The way you make me feel, I know it's written all over me." He leaned down and said the words into her neck as he nipped and sucked at her pulse point. "The way I feel about you, I might as well just go down on you in front of him tomorrow."

She moaned and pushed her ass back into him. She needed him. She needed more of him now.

"I can't hide it much longer, Lucy. How much longer can we pretend that this pussy is his? When we both know exactly whose it is." He finally slid his middle finger into her and she sank down on it gratefully. His thumb stroked across her clit at the same time his finger curled inside her and Lucy's head fell back on his shoulder.

"No. Watch," he said, gently pushing her head back up. Her eyes zeroed in on his hand, slowly pumping into her. "Watch while I remind you whose it is."

She had to blink to focus her eyes through the lust but she was heavily rewarded when she did. She saw a woman with flushed cheeks, eyes heavy, plump lips parted and panting. She saw her full breasts spilling over his arm, one of her nipples peeking out between his fingers. Her curvy waist and full hips pressed back into his hardness as his fingers disappeared inside of her.

His thumb began stroking her in earnest and pleasure came spiraling toward her, just out of reach. He could make her come in fifteen seconds flat, they'd timed it before, but tonight he was intentionally holding her release away, prolonging it.

"Please," she begged, locking eyes with him in the mirror. "Please make me come."

He tipped her forward, placing her palms on the vanity in front of her, bending her over it. Her breasts spilled forward. He jerked out of his pants and shirt and stood there, gloriously naked, behind her. The night shadows of her room puddled in the definition of his muscles. He was so goddamn bulky, almost twice the size of her. It still amazed her that they fit together, that she could take a man of his size.

His eyes broke from hers and in the mirror she watched him study her pussy from behind. His breath came ragged and he shook his head in wonder, assuring her, as always, how much he liked what he saw. He grabbed the base of his cock and dragged the head along her opening, circling her clit and moving back to press into her just an inch. His eyes dragged up and caught hers in the mirror.

"He never gets this, Lucy. This is mine," he said and plunged into her all the way. Lucy kept her eyes open, because she knew he'd want to see it. But her eyes were unseeing as she came. She was spinning through the universe. Every feeling of pleasure he'd ever called out of her rushed back through her, condensed and racing. It was like every orgasm she'd ever had all came to the party at once. She clamped down on him so hard his teeth gritted against it. Her fingers curled into fists as her entire world was just one feeling, one moment. She wasn't a human anymore, she wasn't Lucy, she was just this feeling, this pleasure.

She heard animal, wanton moans in her ears and barely even recognized them as her own. Her muscles felt frozen, locked in place by the ecstasy, but really she was working herself on his cock. Fucking him from the front, she rode out her own orgasm with such sexual energy that he held still behind her, let her work herself through it.

When the feeling finally began to recede, she sagged against the vanity. Resting on her elbows. But this just provided a new angle for him. He gripped her hips so tightly she thought she might bruise, but it felt good. It felt safe and secure. He pulled out almost to the tip and fed himself back into her. Drawing groans from both of them.

"Mine," he ground out through gritted teeth and she turned her cheek to the cool wooden top of the vanity and nodded her head. She pushed her ass back onto him and was pleased at the slapping sound of skin on skin.

"Yes," she moaned. "It's yours, Amos."

The second she said his name, he found his rhythm. He slammed into her over and over, knocking the piece of furniture she leaned on into the wall. Their pants came out in tandem, rough and ragged.

She looked up into the mirror again and saw him staring hard at the place where he entered her. Like he was hypnotized. He was as under the spell of their love making as she was. She dropped her hand to her clit and he pounded into her even faster. He liked it when she played with herself. He always had.

"Oh, you're close, baby. I can tell when you squeeze me like that," he panted as he gripped her hips and rode her faster. And she was close. Watching him rut her like an animal in the mirror had turned her on more than almost anything in her entire life. His face was tight with lust and concentration, the skin over his bulging muscles was damp and glistening. His body pumped into her with feral ferocity.

"Come on it, baby. Come on it," he commanded and she did, just as hard as last time. This time her eyes clamped closed so that nothing would distract her from permanently remembering the feeling of him exploding inside her at the same second. His warmth flooded her womb. She clamped down on him like a fist. He pumped into her fast and deep. Halfway through coming he fell forward, her back to his chest, and he kept pumping into her. His mouth opened on her shoulder and his teeth clamped firmly down. The pain shot to her nipples, and down to her clit which she pinched between her fingers. She was coming from somewhere deep inside her body. Where she didn't even know she could come.

They sagged against one another and the vanity. Completely spent. He picked her up and carried her to the bathroom. He flicked on the taps and put them both in the tub while it was still filling up. She lay on top of him, her back to his front, and looked at the ceiling. She was completely dazed by what just happened. She'd never in her life felt pleasure like that. She hadn't even known it existed.

He reached up and turned off the rushing water after it filled the tub, delightfully warm.

"I'm in love with you," he said. And she was immediately tossed out of her lazy stupor. She tried to turn in his arms to look at him but he pinned her to him so she couldn't move. "I'm so in love with you, Lucy. I'll give you anything you want, hatchling. Anything. You want to find a way to stay here four more years, well I guess I'll figure it out. I'm not crazy about leaving Zara behind either. I'll give you anything you want. But please don't make me share you with him." He pressed his nose into her wet hair and nuzzled her. "It'll kill me dead."

"No one else but you for the rest of my life," she said to the air. This time he let her turn. The deep, moved expression on his face was her undoing. "I'm in love with you too. We'll find a way to keep Zara safe. But not at the expense of him touching me. No one else but you gets to do that for the rest of my life."

He pulled her against him and kissed the breath out of her. Her breasts crushed against his chest as he held her. Her legs floated to either side of his. He dragged her up his body a little further and kissed and sucked her neck.

"I love you," he said, almost tentatively, as if he were experimenting with saying it out loud. He insinuated himself between her legs and thrust into her and at the same second he pushed her down on his cock.

She cried out in pleasure. How was it possible that he just kept making her feel better and better? "I love you," she moaned into his mouth, and started riding him.

CHAPTER FIFTEEN

"Lovebirds. Oh, darling lovebirds," a voice sang.

Lucy felt sleep loosen its grip on her. But she sat up the second she felt Amos's warmth leave her side. She had to blink her eyes at the sight she was seeing. She wasn't sure it was real.

A completely naked Amos stood over the top of someone, his foot crushing the man's windpipe. It was the blonde man she'd often seen in the King's chambers. He'd joined them for part of the day.

"Dude," the blonde man choked out. "I can see your junk."

Amos seemed to press harder on his neck. "What the fuck are you doing here, Oracle."

Ah. So that's who that was. Zara had mentioned something about an oracle here and there, but Lucy would never in a million years have thought this guy was it. He had wavy blonde hair and a kind of surfer vibe about him. He was the only one who hadn't treated the King with complete reverence. He usually seemed as bored by all the proceedings as she was.

The Oracle made a strangled little noise. His face was turning red.

"Amos, you're gonna kill him!" Lucy called from the bed, reaching over to get her robe. She slid it on and came to stand beside him, picking up Amos's pants along the way.

Amos removed his foot from the Oracle's neck and took the pants from Lucy, tugging them on.

"Answer me," Amos bit out. "What the fuck are you doing here."

The Oracle was coughing and holding his throat, but he came to stand. He gestured toward the tousled bed where Amos and Lucy had made love twice more the night before. "I see you've really made your choice then, huh?"

"That's none of your goddamn business," Amos growled, pushing Lucy a little bit behind him.

The Oracle rolled his eyes. "I'm an Oracle, Amos. Everything is my business." He went and flopped down in the armchair on the corner. "Whether I like it or not."

"You mean you can see the future? Our future?" Lucy asked, and stepped forward. Amos reached out and grabbed the back of her robe, tugging her back to his front.

"Not exactly. There isn't one future." The Oracle examined his fingernails as he spoke. "There's lots of possibilities, depending on the decisions people make. But I gotta say you two have really made your decision."

"What's that supposed to mean?" Lucy snapped. Something about the Oracle was kind of annoying. Amos stroked a hand over her shoulder as if he were saying, *just ignore it, I know this guy's a douche.*

"It means you fanned the flames, you dirty lovebirds." The Oracle flashed a lascivious grin and bit at a hangnail. "Don't get me wrong. I'm a fan of this. I never wanted the King to have you, Lucy."

"You're the one who tracked her down and brought her here!" Amos growled.

The Oracle rolled his eyes. "If she had simply been a perfect genetic match for the King, I never would have brought her here. I would have lied. I'd never condemn a woman to a fate as unthinkable as that."

"Then why the fuck did you bring her here?" Amos's voice was almost unrecognizable with anger.

The Oracle leaned his head on one of his palms. Outwardly he looked bored, but Lucy could see nerves lick across his face. "I don't serve the King, Amos."

Amos stepped around Lucy so fast she couldn't even follow it with her eyes. His hands shot out and his dragon claws appeared. Amos raised one arm to swipe across the Oracle's neck. But the Oracle raised his hand and spoke.

"And neither do you anymore, Amos. Remember that."

Amos froze. Lucy froze. The Oracle froze.

"Will somebody please explain this to me?" Lucy yelled. "I'm a little in the dark over here."

Amos snicked his claws closed and tore a hand through his hair.

"Who the fuck do you serve then, Oracle."

"You know who I'm talking about." The Oracle said, biting his fingernail again.

"Fuck," Amos growled. "FUCK."

"Who?" Lucy exclaimed, still totally confused.

"Solar," Amos bit out, beyond agitated.

"Who the hell is Solar?" Lucy was just as agitated as he was right about then.

Amos paced back and forth. The Oracle leaned around him so that he could see Lucy. "Well, pretty much in a nutshell, Solar is a kid Amos grew up with.

They were best friends until Solar decided to head up a rebel alliance that's trying to overthrow the King."

Lucy's jaw dropped open. Holy shit. And he'd never even mentioned it?

"He's still my best friend." There was murder in Amos's eyes but Lucy had no idea who it was even for, the Oracle, this Solar guy, or himself. Amos turned to Lucy. "He's like a brother to me. But when he decided that he couldn't live under the King's rule, we had to part ways." He brought his hand roughly through his hair. "Or risk having to kill one another."

"Wow, stunner," the Oracle said in such a way that Lucy knew he already knew that whole story. He leaned back around to see Lucy.

"Anyhow, I just revealed to Amos that I'm a member of that alliance as well. And right now Amos's DNA is telling him to murder me for treason. Hence, the claws and the, you know, insanely intense anger." He gestured to Amos's tight demeanor.

"But basically, he's grappling with that because he's ALSO not loyal to the King anymore because of your pretty little ass. And I think that pretty much brings you back up to speed." The Oracle leaned back in his chair as if he were exhausted.

"You brought her here because you knew how much she would mean to me," Amos said tightly, putting the pieces together.

The Oracle nodded.

"You knew when you found her that she's the only thing that would tear me away from guarding the King," Amos continued.

"And you and the alliance needed Amos out of the way to be able to get to the King," Lucy cut in.

Again the Oracle nodded. "Pretty much, yeah. You guys got it right on the nose."

"Wow." Lucy plunked herself onto the bed. "Wow."

"Is she even a genetic match for the King?" Amos asked, his voice rising. "Or did you just bring her here to fuck with me and destroy the entire monarchy?"

"Oh no. Trust me. She'd breed strong with the King. But a lot of women would." He looked her up and down before adding more. "But I have to say, your girl is an especially fertile one. She could mate with a rock and create a hatchling. We SUPER don't want the King to knock her up. That would be bad news all around."

Amos growled and threw his hands up in the air. Obviously torn between hating the Oracle and agreeing with his last statement.

The Oracle stood. "Which is why I'm here to help you."

"How?" Lucy snapped, her nerves pulled tight like a bow string.

"Look, this whole 'four more years, hide in the realm, and then rescue Zara mess' you guys have planned is bullshit. It's gonna get you both killed."

Again, Lucy's jaw dropped. "How did you..." she trailed off.

"Oracle," the Oracle reminded her, pointing at himself. "I see alllllllllllll." He waved his hands in front of his face. "Sometimes too much. Seriously, you guys need to give it a rest sometimes. Some of us are trying to sleep around here."

"Jesus Christ," Amos threw his hands in the air and paced away, obviously trying to put space between him and the Oracle.

"Get to the part about you helping us," Lucy said.

"Oh, right. Well, basically, the night of the harvest moon, the alliance is going to break into the fortress and create a major distraction that will allow you guys to get through the portal without anybody noticing."

"What major distraction?" Amos asked, his arms crossed over his chest like a vice.

"Well, we can't try to assassinate the King while you're still in this realm because it'll trigger your super protection bodyguard mode thing you have going on. And we're not dumb. We know we can't compete with that. So that's out."

"Then what is it?" Lucy asked, totally exasperated.

"We're gonna kidnap Zara."

His statement was met with complete silence as Amos and Lucy's brains whirred, trying to see the plan from different angles.

"What are you gonna do with her?" Lucy asked.

The Oracle's voice softened a little bit. "Look, she's a good kid. And she's been dealt a shit hand. Amos and Solar have known her since we was born, practically."

Amos nodded, confirming.

"Solar feels like a brother to her. He doesn't want her to be condemned to being one of the King's wives. So he wants to kidnap her from here and take her away, someplace that the King can't get to her."

"And while he's at it, he can use her as a bargaining chip," Amos muttered.

"What do you mean?" the Oracle asked.

"She's the King's favorite wife," Amos said. "Sorry, hatchling." He flashed her a grin that she had to meet.

"Anyway," he continued. "The King would probably do almost anything to get Zara back. It'll help draw him out."

The Oracle's jaw dropped in what seemed to be genuine surprise. "Are you helping make a plan for the rebel alliance? Even I did not see that coming."

Amos dropped down onto the bed next to Lucy. She could feel the overwhelming tension roll off of him.

"The harvest moon is in two days. Are you guys prepared?" Lucy asked the Oracle.

"We are, especially if Amos isn't going to block our plans."

Amos held still, his silence an acquiescence to the Oracle's words.

"It'll happen at dinnertime. Be ready to leave."

"Fine," Amos snapped. "Get the fuck out of here."

The Oracle stood and rolled his hand in front of him in a fancy bow. "Pleasure as always."

CHAPTER SIXTEEN

Amos clenched his jaw as he waited for the big distraction to come. It was two days later and dinner had gone on for twenty minutes already. He could see the harvest moon out the window of the great dining room. The portal was open and the King was ready to mate. Amos's nerves were a wreck.

The King had chained Lucy's hand to his own in the traditional consummation night jewelry. The cuff was the same gold of the one around her neck. Lucy sat at the head of the table, next to the King, and Amos could see her disgusted expression from across the hall.

This was torture. The meal was cleared away and Amos was sure he was going to lose his mind. After the dessert course the King was sure to take Lucy back to his chambers. Amos's fists clenched.

The Oracle caught his eye across the room. He was telling him to calm down. Amos knew that. But then King Dalyer stood up, raising his goblet. Lucy had to stand as well because of the shackle around her wrist. The wives raised their goblets. Their bodyguards, Amos, and the Oracle were the only other people in the room.

Come on, Solar. Amos thought. *Any minute now.*

The King cleared his throat. "Thank you for being here on this very special consummation night. The night of the harvest moon. This is especially important to me, because the Oracle assures me that this is the night this wife will conceive the most powerful heir my family line has ever known."

Amos noticed Zara looking queasy. He wished they could have let her in on the secret. But they weren't sure she wouldn't have given it away.

"In honor of this special night," King Dalyer said, his eyes darkening. "I'm instituting primal law."

Amos's blood froze. He saw the Oracle's face go white as a sheet. How the fuck could he not have seen this.

"No!" Zara yelled.

Lucy looked around, totally confused. She didn't know that primal law meant the King was going to take her right then and there. Publicly. So there was no questioning that she carried his child, the heir to the throne.

The King pushed Lucy to floor, and not expecting it, she easily toppled. Amos felt something come loose inside of him. It was like an egg hatching. Something he'd been incubating for a long time finally came of age. An primal, ancient scream ripped out of his throat and everyone turned to stare at him as he shifted. Immediately full dragon.

King Dalyer looked up. "Amos. I knew you lusted after this woman, but to take it this far..." the King shook his head in fascinated disgust.

He unclipped himself from Lucy who immediately slid away as the King started his disgustingly wet shift.

The wives scattered as the King cuffed the dining table to one side. It smashed on the wall of the great hall as the two dragons squared off. The bodyguards lining the walls looked between Amos and King Dalyer in confusion. Two dragons they never thought they'd see fight were whipping their tails at one another and roaring with rage.

Out of the corner of his eye, Amos saw the Oracle usher Lucy and the wives to one end of the great hall. But that was the last thing he noticed about the room before he lunged at the King.

Sorry, ancestors. He was about to destroy the royal line.

His humongous jaw sank into the King's shoulder and Dalyer gave a roar loud enough to shake the chandeliers. Amos drew back and stomped one of his mighty back legs straight to the King's chest, flinging him across the room.

The duty inside a few of the bodyguards apparently woke up because suddenly Amos wasn't facing off just one dragon, he was facing off three. One of them circled around to his blind spot and rose up in flight, trying to immobilize Amos from the air. Amos swung his tail without looking and plunged the vicious spike on the end through the guard's wing. He didn't want to kill these men.

Only the King.

Amos lunged at the King again, but the other two bodyguards got in the way, flinging him backwards. But they were no match for him. Amos burst through their wall and grabbed hold of the King with his front claws.

He picked the older dragon up as if he were a rag doll and tossed him fully into the wall. The great hall shook. King Dalyer stood, a wicked glint in his eyes, and Amos knew what he was going to do before he did it.

The King's main weapon wasn't his size or speed. It was the poisonous spikes he could shoot from his mouth.

Amos was prepared to turn his scales to the poison. It couldn't harm him unless it got in his mouth or eyes. But a sickening second later, he realized that he wasn't where the King was aiming.

In his vindictiveness, his willingness to completely and utterly destroy an enemy, the King was willing to destroy his own future. He always had been. That viciousness was one of the reasons he had retained the throne for so long as an older dragon with no heir. He used that viciousness now. And aimed the poison at the wives.

At Lucy.

Amos felt the claws of the other dragons dig into him. One set of them on his shoulder and one on his haunches. But the pain meant nothing to him. It was nothing compared to the thing that was exploding inside of him. The worst, most powerful pain he'd ever felt was rising up in him. He felt it come straight from his belly and up out of his throat. He tasted rage, fear, and mortality in what was ripping up through him.

He tasted the pain he wanted the King to feel. But most of all, he tasted his love for Lucy, and everything he would do to protect her. He opened his mouth to roar and a thirty foot long stream of red hot fire exploded out of him. It incinerated the poison darts in midair. It blew a hole through the rock wall beyond. It instantly hiked the temperature in the hall by thirty degrees.

Amos thought only of Lucy as he turned the spray toward the King, ready to extinguish him from the world.

But he heard Lucy cry out from behind him. He shut his mouth on the fire and turned. The roof of the great hall trembled and quaked as it suddenly was being lifted at the corners. At least ten dragons kicked and clawed, crumbling the roof into the great hall.

Amos locked eyes with a midnight blue dragon he recognized well. Solar.

Amos's job wasn't to fight anymore. It was to run. With Lucy. He turned on his haunches and realized he could be quicker in his human form. Transforming on the fly, he sprinted across the hall as a human.

Lucy saw him coming and turned to run along his side, gripping his hand. As they passed, Amos watched Solar land beside Zara and toss one of the velvet tapestries around her so his scales wouldn't hurt her. He picked her up in his humongous arms and lifted off into the air, that part of the plan complete.

Lucy and Amos sprinted out of the great hall and down a narrow corridor. Lucy had no idea how to get to the portal so Amos shouted directions as they went.

He could hear someone else's footsteps pounding behind him, but when he looked it was just the Oracle.

"Dude, congrats!" the Oracle yelled.

"On what?" Lucy yelled back.

"On the whole true mate thing!"

"What?!" Lucy screeched.

"I summoned fire," Amos said as they crashed into the nondescript cellar that held the entrance to the portal. He turned to her and ran a hand over her head.

She nodded. "Which you said dragons can only do to protect their true mate." Her brow furrowed. She whirled and looked at the Oracle. "Which means I'm pregnant?!"

"I told you that you were fertile myrtle," the Oracle said, grinning at her and holding his arms out for a hug.

Amos and Lucy hugged one another instead.

"Oh my god," Amos said into her hair over and over again. But then he looked up, glaring into the Oracle's face.

"You told me that dragons could only get humans pregnant on the harvest moon."

The Oracle's mouth dropped open. "And you believed me?! That's just some shit I told the King to buy the alliance some more time after Lucy got here."

Amos and Lucy had twin flabbergasted looks pasted across their faces.

The Oracle covered his mouth with one hand. "Holy shit, have you guys been barebacking it because you thought she couldn't get pregnant? Wow. My bad, you guys. My bad."

Lucy put her face in her hands and a little half laugh, a half sob came out. "You know, it's kind of ok."

The ground above them shook and a roar from overhead got them scrambling.

"The King," Amos said, tugging Lucy toward the portal.

"Amos," the Oracle said. "You're gonna have to destroy the portal once you're through."

"What? I can't do that! That would destroy the tie between the two realms."

"Trust me. There's another one. And if the King gets down here before it's destroyed he's gonna come through. And there are more women he could successfully breed with on earth. He can't get through."

Amos raked his hand through his hair as the ground shook again. The King was almost there.

"How do I destroy it?" he asked the Oracle.

"With your love fire, baby." The Oracle grinned and waggled his eyebrows. "I'll come and find you guys soon. You won't have to stay on earth forever if you don't want to raise your little guy there."

They heard a roar right outside the door and Lucy quickly hugged the Oracle before Amos grabbed her around the waist and launched them through the blackhole.

CHAPTER SEVENTEEN

This time was decidedly not as bad, Lucy realized. She was snuggled up against Amos's chest and she didn't think she was coming face to face with death. She was going home, back to earth. And the thought was enough to comfort her through the debilitating nothingness of going through the portal.

They landed with a thud on the floor of the abandoned subway station. Amos shielded her body with his. But as soon as they landed he was transforming back into his dragon form to summon the fire that was going to destroy the portal. Right before he opened his mighty mouth, a small little bundle flew through, hitting Lucy gently on the belly.

Then Amos was roaring and lighting up the long dingy track with a fireball that trumped his first. The inky black portal exploded like an oil fire over the ocean. For a second, it almost looked like the portal was going to consume the fire, but Amos kept it coming. Suddenly, the portal collapsed in on itself.

And then air was just the air. Dingy and singed from the fire. Lucy looked down at the bundle in her arms and chuckled when she realized what it was. Amos transformed back into his human form and came to help her stand.

"What are you laughing at?" he asked.

"The Oracle threw his shoes and pants through the portal for you."

Confusedly Amos looked down at his naked body. "Wow, that was actually pretty nice of him." He grabbed the pants and tugged them on. "Wait, did I run through the fortress completely naked just now?"

Lucy bit her lip and tried not to smile. "Yup."

He tied on the shoes and took Lucy's hand. This time she led the way.

"Are you gonna teach me how to be human?" he asked, overwhelmed with the thought of trying to fit in to the human world until the Oracle came to retrieve them.

"Never," she said, looking back at him through the dark. "I love your dragon way too much."

EPILOGUE

Lucy rolled her eyes as she heard the downstairs broomstick bang against her floor again. She knew it would only be a matter of minutes before Ms. Tisdale came stomping up the stairs to yell again. They used to be such good friends before Lucy ever went to the dragon realm. But now...

Bang. Bang. Bang. Ms. Tisdale rattled the door on the hinges and Lucy shot Amos a meaningful look over her shoulder. He gingerly gathered up the tiny dragon making all the noise and carried him to their bedroom, shutting the door.

Lucy opened the door to their apartment. "Yes, Ms. Tisdale?"

"Lucy, you know I like children," she started without preamble. "And god knows I like that husband of yours. So helpful around here with all the repairs."

Lucy struggled not to roll her eyes. Ms. Tisdale certainly liked to WATCH Amos do repairs. "Uh huh," she said, already knowing what came next.

"But your boy is just too loud. He bangs my ceiling day and night. And that yell! Goodness, it's like a lion roaring up here."

"A dragon," Lucy corrected.

"Excuse me?"

"When he's roaring it's because he's being a dragon."

"Sure, of course, I'm sure he has a beautiful imagination. Dear, I say this from the bottom of my heart. But sometimes he's such a little monster."

Lucy sucked her lips in and tried not to laugh. "Ms. Tisdale, you have no idea."

Lucy said goodbye and shut the door on Ms. Tisdale. She went back and flung open the door to their bedroom. Two year old Drake came barreling across the hardwood floors straight to his mama's arms.

Predictably not in control of his shift at age two, everything from head to toe was human except for the little baby dragon tail sprouting from his rump.

"Yowza," Lucy said, giving her boy a squeeze and then sending him skittering back toward his Papa. "His scales are starting to get prickly."

"They won't get full sharpness until he's five," Amos said.

"That's just cruel. Can you imagine a five year old who can't fully control his shift with sharp scales? That seems like a serious design flaw, dragonkind."

"Nah, the sharpness helps you learn how to control your shift when you're a kid. You get tired of scraping yourself." Amos reached up and pulled his wife down on his lap. "You need more rest. And food. And water. And juice."

"We're doing fine," Lucy said, pressing a hand to her rounding belly. They'd found out a month ago that they had another on the way. "What I really need is to make love with my husband."

They turned and looked at Drake, trying to gauge how far out they were from nap time. He was dancing from foot to foot, swiping blocks aside with his dragon tail.

Amos sighed. "I'll fuck you tonight, hatchling. I promise."

Lucy was just leaning in for a kiss, when another knock came on their apartment door. "Jeez Louise, give it rest, Ms. Tisdale."

Amos firmly planted a hand under his wife's ass and helped heave her into a standing position. Lucy knew that had been something he'd loved about her first pregnancy, how many times he'd had to lift and carry her while she got used to the weight of carrying a dragon egg in her womb. Much denser than a human baby. She knew he was looking forward to it with this pregnancy as well.

Lucy schooled her face into a tolerant expression and pulled open the door, expecting to go toe to toe with Ms. Tisdale. But her face dropped into one of pure surprise when she saw the Oracle leaning against the door jamb.

"Barefoot and pregnant really suits you," he grinned at her.

Amos was immediately padding into the living room as soon as he heard a man's voice instead of Ms. Tisdale's, Drake on his hip. He stopped cold the second he saw the Oracle there.

Much to Lucy and Amos's surprise, Drake instantly held out his arms for the Oracle.

"Wow," Lucy said. "He doesn't usually like strangers."

"I'm not a stranger," the Oracle said, walking into the apartment and holding out his arms for the baby. "We had plenty of chats while he was getting ready to hatch. I really had to talk this guy out of the egg." He turned back to a stunned Lucy and Amos. "You're welcome for that, by the way. He wanted to stay in a whole other week."

"You're really gonna have to explain how your gift works someday," Lucy said, sitting on the couch next to Amos.

"Trust me," the Oracle said. "You don't wanna know."

Still the same old Amos, he cut to the chase. "Are you here to bring us back?"

The Oracle made a high pitched sort of noise and nodded his head from side to side. "I mean, eventually. But I have something I need you guys to do first."

Lucy leaned back and crossed her arms over her chest, smiling when she found Amos in the same position.

"Oh really," she said.

The Oracle nodded toward their blank TV screen and they all turned to look. It blinked on and frenetically scrolled through channels as the Oracle shuffled through his mind for what he was looking for.

"You've gotta find this man and convince him to come to the dragon realm."

The screen went dark and then lit up on a man's face. His long dark hair fell in waves to his shoulders. Light eyes were shaded under a hand as he looked out at something in the bright light. His sharp jaw was stubbled.

"Uh, yum," Lucy said and grinned cheekily up at her scowling husband.

"Who is he?" Amos asked.

"I actually don't know," the Oracle said, leaning back in the chair.

Amos and Lucy looked at one another in surprise. The Oracle actually looked a little frustrated. Something they'd never seen before.

"There's some kind of block around him. I don't know anything about him. All I know is that the revolution has stalled. We can't go any further and every time I search for answers, all roads lead to this guy."

Amos scratched at his chin, trying to be casual. "What do you mean the revolution has stalled? Is Solar alright?"

"Yeah," the Oracle nodded. "Solar is good. If not a little grumpy. I don't know if he anticipated babysitting Zara quite so much after they rescued her from Dalyer."

Lucy leaned forward, so relieved to hear that Zara was doing alright.

"But Solar's good. It's Dalyer. He's holed himself up somewhere in the mountains. Even I can't find him. Yet he's still able to send messages to his troops who are ravaging the countryside. We need help. And I think this guy is it. I can't give you his exact coordinates, but I know he's out in the Coeur D'Alene area."

Amos nodded, taking it all in. "I think we can probably do that for you."

Lucy shrugged. "It has gotten tricky, raising a dragon in Brooklyn. Might be time for a change of scenery. Maybe a little more space for the kids." She patted her belly.

"Although, it comes at a price," Amos said.

"What?" the Oracle asked suspiciously.

"We'll do it. As long as you stay and babysit while I have my way with my wife." With that, Amos stood up and snagged Lucy's hand. Dragging her toward the bedroom. She laughed in delight and stumbled along with him.

"Extortionists!" the Oracle hollered after them. "You're lucky I like your son so much! And you're having a girl by the way!"

Amos shut the door on him and turned to Lucy. Tears had filled her eyes.

"A girl," she whispered holding her hands out to him.

"A girl," he whispered back, his voice filled with wonder. "I hope she has your eyes."

"I hope she has your heart," Lucy said. Then thinking more, "And your poisonous tail spike. That would really come in handy with any over-frisky boyfriends."

Laughing, they fell to the mattress together. Kissing, and rolling, and becoming one.

THE END

Printed in Poland
by Amazon Fulfillment
Poland Sp. z o.o., Wrocław